TWO
CRIMES

By the same author

THE DEAD GIRLS

A NOVEL BY **Jorge Ibargüengoitia**

TRANSLATED BY **Asa Zatz**

CHATTO & WINDUS · THE HOGARTH PRESS
LONDON

TWO
CRIMES

Published in 1984 by
Chatto & Windus · The Hogarth Press
40 William IV Street, London WC2N 4DF

First published in Spanish by Editorial Joaquin Moritz, Mexico, 1979

ISBN 0 7011 2816 x Hardback
ISBN 0 7011 2817 8 Paperback

Printed and bound in Great Britain by
Redwood Burn Limited, Trowbridge, Wiltshire

TWO

CRIMES

PART ONE

chios, looked like a dark-brown mountain stuck on the three-legged stool. There were three figures on the shocking-pink couch: Olga Pereira, tall, slender, in blue jeans, lying next to the wall, eyes fixed on the ceiling; gray-haired Lidia Reynoso, oldest of the group, wearing an orange-colored quechquemitl, settled down alongside Olga's bare feet, listening incredulously to Pancho; at the opposite end of the couch, by Olga's head, Manuel Rodríguez, curled up, trying to read under the reddish lamplight Poliakov's *Critique of the Capitalist State*, which he had pulled out of the bookshelf. Carlos Pereira, who fancied himself another Che Guevara (whose portrait hung on the wall), was rocking himself in a rustic wooden chair, smoking a cigar. Poised on her celebrated ass encased in dark-green trousers and spilling over the edges of the seat, was Ifigenia, busily arranging her hair.

The Chamuca, guitar in hand, appeared at the bedroom door and looked at me fleetingly. I understood that she had decided to sing in order to put an end to the irritating discussion and Pancho's imbecilities. I applauded, and all the others, except Pancho, followed suit. The Chamuca, stretching out her long legs carefully so as not to step on anybody, made her way between the guests to perch on the edge of the couch. She had taken off her huipil, remaining in the embroidered cotton waist I had asked her not to use in public because her nipples, which are very dark, showed through. She tuned up her guitar and, paying no attention to the requests being called out, struck a resounding chord and launched into her favorite song, "Portrait of Carlos Macías, the Guerrillero."

It is difficult for me to describe my feelings when the Chamuca sings. To begin with, I am proud that such a beautiful woman should belong to me. She is dark-skinned, has very large eyes, full lips, magnificent

1

The story I am going to tell begins on a night the police violated the Constitution. It was the same night the Chamuca and I threw a party to celebrate the fifth anniversary, not of our wedding, because we aren't married, but of the thirteenth of April, the day she "gave herself to me" on one of the drafting tables in the government Planning Office. A dense dust storm had blotted out even the Monument to the Revolution two blocks away. I was a draftsman. The Chamuca had studied sociology but her appointment was as a stenographer. The two of us had been working overtime and there was no one else in the office. We invited six of our closest friends to our apartment for the anniversary party. Five of them arrived before eight o'clock loaded with presents, "Paws" bringing the Lukacs book, the Pereiras a Santa Marta poncho, Lidia Reynoso dishes from Tzinzunzan, and Manuel Rodríguez two bottles of real vodka he had gotten through a friend who worked at the Soviet embassy.

The gathering started out as one of the most enjoyable I ever attended, all of us talking, drinking, laughing, and singing like one happy family. "Paws" had just gotten home from a vacation at the seaside. He described a remote little place where there were no tourists, that had a beach of fine white sand, a cove of the most transparent water, and clams fresh out of the ocean. I wanted to know how to get there and he wrote the directions for me in my address book: *Take launch that runs from port of Ticomán to Half Moon Beach (Aurora Hotel).* Little did I realize what that note was to signify for me.

The Chamuca served the tamale pie at eleven o'clock. We were eating it when the sixth guest, Ifigenia Trejo, arrived bringing a stranger. The instant he crossed the threshold, the party chilled as though a cold shower had suddenly fallen on us. Ifigenia introduced him as "Pancho" and us as "some friends."

I sensed something fishy about Pancho as soon as I set eyes on him, with his gold tooth, double chin, suit, shirt, and necktie. The first thing he did after shaking hands with us was to ask to use the bathroom. As soon as he was gone, I turned to Ifigenia, who was sitting down in one of the rush chairs, and asked, "Who is this guy?"

"He works for the Department of Justice."

"Why did you bring him here?"

"Because he wanted to meet you people."

There weren't enough plates to go around, so the Chamuca had to use two of the Tzinzunzan dishes for serving the tamale pie to those who had just arrived. When Pancho returned from the bathroom, he removed his jacket, sat down beside Ifigenia, and, instead of eating his food, rested the plate on one of the bookcases, preferring to drink the Cuba libre I offered him. He downed it nonstop, accepted a second, and fixed himself a third without asking. When Lidia Reynoso stood up to serve herself dessert—there was coconut custard—he took advantage of the opportunity to vacate the rush chair he was in and flop into the place she had been occupying on the lilac-colored cushion, the most comfortable seat in the room. No sooner was he installed, legs folded under him, than he began to spout stupidities, saying that socialism is a dogma, Marxism should no longer be considered a valid political doctrine since it does not take into account the power of which is innate in the human being, and so on.

"If you are going to get started now on Stalin the concentration camps in the Soviet Union," Olga Pereira, "wake me up when you're finished." that she stretched out on the couch, lying on her to flaunt her contempt for Pancho.

Lidia Reynoso, unable to believe her ears, mut to me, "But this man is an anti-Marxist!"

Pancho was asking why, if socialism was such fect system, people emigrated from the socialist tries, and how it was that nobody wanted to g live in the Soviet Union. The Chamuca, fists cle under her huipil, replied, "You are mistaken, Many people move to the Soviet Union from all The only difference is that they do it without the licity that the defectors from socialism get."

Having said this, she rose and left the room. "I moved his stool to a point directly in front of P and with infinite patience began explaining to hir difficult it was to eradicate the petit bourgeois in from man.

Ifigenia had loosened her hair and was making It is her custom. If she happens to be wearing a po when she arrives at a party, she makes braids; comes with braids, she undoes them, brushes the and goes home with a ponytail. In either case, she behind four or five unmistakable long, thick, very hairs as a souvenir. I was watching her with her upraised, her mouth filled with hairpins, and re that she was embarrassed by the imbecilities her panion was uttering . . . but not embarrassed en I regretted having invited her.

Pancho, in a white shirt, held a green glass hand. "Paws," tugging at his Zapatista-style n teeth, wears big hoop earrings, and is built like a monument to our race. She is also a little ridiculous. When she sings she opens her mouth wide, screws up her eyes, and lets out howls of bogus emotion. It makes me uncomfortable but I bear with it because I believe that people are entitled to express themselves as best they can. That's my philosophy.

When I recall that scene of the Chamuca singing, with me looking at her and the others listening, it astonishes me to think how far removed I was then from conceiving that this was to be our last night in the house and that the image of the ill-fated party would stick in my mind as the most vivid and painful remembrance of our beloved apartment on Miguel Schultz Street or that the shocking-pink couch, the Havana Festival posters, and the bookcases the Chamuca and I had built with our own hands would, on being called to memory, seem to be not the everyday objects that made up part of a happy life but the elements of a stage setting for that disastrous gathering.

The Chamuca sang several songs and her purpose was achieved. Pancho not only stopped talking, but fell asleep. She was in the middle of "Guajira Patrol" when there was a knock on the door.

I thought it must be one of the neighbors coming to complain because it was after one in the morning. To my surprise there was nobody there when I opened the door. I looked down the hall and a few meters away could make out the figure of a short man, his hands in his pockets. It was very dark in that hall—the landlady puts in twenty-watt bulbs—so it took a moment before I recognized the gloomy face of Evodio Alcocer.

The thought of another uninvited guest arriving at that hour did not fill me with cheer. That it should be Evodio, even less. I have respect for Evodio because I know him to be a dedicated activist, but I do not share his convictions, he does not belong to my group, and I have very little in common with him. Nonetheless, I said to him, "Evodio, how nice to see you. Come in."

He didn't move. He just remained standing there in the hall looking like a statue of Benito Juárez. Finally, he raised his hand and made a sign for me to approach. I shut the apartment door so the neighbors wouldn't hear "Guajira Patrol" and went over to him. His eyes were red, his lips pursed.

"Are you giving a party?" he asked, as though he considered it a bad idea for me to be doing so.

The Chamuca's voice was echoing through the hall.

"It's a lively party," I told him. "Why don't you come in?"

"Who's inside?"

I don't know why the question shouldn't have struck me as rude, but I guess it didn't because I answered him amiably, naming all the guests, including Pancho, whom I described as "a friend of Ifigenia Trejo's." He peered down at the mottled green tile floor as he listened and when I had finished the enumeration, he shrugged and said, "I guess it's okay."

"What's okay?"

Instead of answering my question, which would have saved us a lot of headaches, he said, "I am going to ask a very big favor of you. Let me spend the night in your house."

When somebody asks me for a favor in such a direct manner, I can hardly ever bring myself to refuse, but at the same time I don't like to say yes, just like that. I would have preferred to know for what reason Evodio wanted to stay overnight in my apartment but I wasn't on intimate enough terms with him to ask what was preventing him from going home to sleep. I assumed he was having a matrimonial problem—he was married to a neurotic Argentinian woman he had met in Moscow—so I said to him, "Sure, you can stay overnight, Evodio."

We entered the room together in a very natural way as though Evodio was invited but had been delayed in getting to the party. This fiction did not go over because everybody there, except Pancho, knew Evodio as well, or as little, as I did, which was sufficient for them to be aware that he was not part of our group, never attended our parties, and must be in some sort of trouble to be arriving at such an hour. The Chamuca put down her guitar and greeted Evodio with an embrace and exclamations that left no doubt as to the unexpectedness of his visit. Pancho woke up.

"Hungry, Evodio?" the Chamuca asked.

"Yes," said Evodio.

The Chamuca went to the kitchen to heat up the tamale pie.

"Sit over here, Evodio," said Lidia Reynoso, patting the seat the Chamuca had vacated.

Evodio sat and I handed him a Cuba libre. Pancho, who had been observing him, said, "We haven't been introduced."

"The gentleman's name is Evodio Alcocer," Lidia Reynoso said.

That was the one indiscretion. Pancho gave his name, to which nobody paid the slightest attention, and held out his hand to Evodio.

After the Chamuca had given Evodio his plate and he was eating voraciously, the other guests began to get to their feet, stretching cramped muscles and ferreting out their misplaced belongings from under the furniture: Olga Pereira, a shoe; Ifigenia Trejo, a red ribbon; Lidia Reynoso, an embroidered Otomi carrying bag. Then a minor tragedy occurred. On reaching for his jacket, Pancho knocked the Tzinzunzan dish off the bookcase, breaking it. He apologized to the Cha muca but let me pick up the fragments and take them to the kitchen. When I returned to the living room, Lidia Reynoso was almost in tears. "They don't make plates like those any more," she said to me.

"I'm sure we'll be able to glue it together," I said consolingly, even though I had already thrown the pieces into the garbage pail.

I had to accompany the guests downstairs to let them out because Estefanita, the janitress, always double-locked the entrance door at night. When I returned to the apartment, the Chamuca was gathering up the dirty glasses.

"Where's Evodio?" I asked.

She made a motion in the direction of the bathroom.

"He's going to spend the night here," I said.

"He told me."

"I had no choice. I hope you don't mind."

"Not too much," she said, and left the room carrying the tray of glasses.

Not only was Evodio going to sleep over, but the Chamuca was now in a bad mood. To mollify her I helped her clean up and pile the dirty dishes in the sink. The Chamuca got the bedding out of the closet and made up the couch for Evodio. When he emerged from the bathroom, he announced, "I have a headache."

The Chamuca went to the bedroom for an aspirin and I brought him a glass of water from the kitchen. After Evodio had swallowed the pill, we showed him where the light switch was and said goodnight. When I went into the bathroom, I was met by the smell Evodio's shit had left behind, and opened the window. I looked down on the deserted street. There was nothing to be seen but papers scattered all about and, in the light of the streetlamp, the sign over the shop across the way that said *Casa Domínguez, Rubber Stamps*.

When I entered the bedroom, I found the Chamuca

leaning over the bed, naked, removing the bedspread. I recall that this excited me greatly and that I began to fondle her ass, but she rejected me.

"No," she said, "Evodio will hear us."

That wouldn't have stopped me, but the fact remained that he would, indeed, have been able to hear us because the head of the couch was against the wall. We went to bed and I turned out the light. The bell in the church on San Cosme Avenue struck three. I fell asleep immediately.

I woke up under the impression that I was sober, but didn't remember about Evodio until I came into the living room and saw him there asleep on the couch. He was in his underwear, lying on his back, a fly poised on his lip. The room smelled to high heaven. I opened the window on the airshaft and went into the bathroom. My beard, which I had begun growing three years before and to which I was quite accustomed by now, startled me. After showering, I looked out of the window. A street cleaner in his orange-colored uniform was pushing his cart, and the proprietor of Casa Domínguez was raising the metal curtain of his shop. I felt depressed. How I wished Evodio would be on his way!

I went back to the bedroom and awakened the Chamuca, it being time for her to get up to go to work. She stood drowsily and was about to walk out of the room naked.

"Don't forget, Evodio's asleep in the living room," I warned her.

That roused her completely. She threw me a look filled with rancor and put on her bathrobe.

"Evodio is more your friend than mine," I reminded her.

"But I didn't invite him to stay over," she pointed out, and left the room.

With the kitchen full of dirty dishes and Evodio asleep

in the living room, it was impossible to have breakfast at home. I was on the verge of waking him up and telling him it was urgent that he go, but decided it would be finer to leave a note. After putting on my Argentine boots, I got a sheet of paper and wrote:

> *Dear Evodio,*
> *It is 8:30 and we are dashing off to work. You'll find things for breakfast in the refrigerator. Eat whatever you want. Don't worry about washing the dishes or making the bed.*
> *So long, with embraces, from*
> *Marcos and the Chamuca*

With this, I thought we would be rid of him. As the Chamuca was opening the apartment door, I put the note on the little table beside the couch so that Evodio could not avoid seeing it as soon as he was up. I then joined the Chamuca and we locked up as quietly as possible.

We had breakfast in a lunchroom on Ejido Street opposite the Planning Office. As the waitress was serving my coffee with hot milk, I caught a glimpse of the headlines on the newspaper—I think it was *La Prensa*—the man at a neighboring table was reading. It said: "FIRST GLOBO ARSONIST ARRESTED." El Globo was a department store that had been burned down three or four months before. The case had received a lot of notoriety but was not solved. I reflected on this for a moment and then forgot about it.

We walked out into the sun and I felt very warm. I did not realize until that moment that I was wearing the Santa Marta poncho the Pereiras had given us the night before. The Chamuca, who understood why I was looking so surprised, said to me, "You're drunk."

She had dark circles under her eyes, but I made no

comment. We crossed Ejido Street against the traffic and went running into the building of the Planning Office. It was just nine when we punched in. The Chamuca got off the elevator at the fourth floor practically without a parting word to me. She was still angry. I continued on to the sixth floor, hung up my poncho on the clothes rack next to the drafting-room door, sat down at my drawing table, and lit a cigarette. I had very little work to do and even less desire to do it. I sat looking out of the window observing the Monument to the Revolution from nine until eleven o'clock when I was called to the telephone. It took a moment for me to recognize the voice at the other end as belonging to Estefanita, the janitress of our building. She sounded agitated as she said, "I have this news for you, señor Marcos, that four men from the government came looking for you. They wanted to know where you and the señora were and that I should open the apartment. I thought it would be empty so I let them in and they took away the señor who was sleeping in the living room in his underwear. They asked me where you and the señora work and, señor Marcos, I swear I told them I didn't know, but I think they are going to be there pretty soon looking for you. I'm telling you so you can be prepared."

"Thanks a lot, Estefanita," I told her, and hung up. And so that portion of my life came to a close.

Not for a moment did the thought enter my mind, or the Chamuca's, that if a person is innocent he has nothing to fear. We certainly were innocent, but the Chamuca had a record of participation in demonstrations, I am *remiso*, that is to say, I never registered for military service, and both of us have been in contact with militant socialist groups. Besides, we were well aware that if it suited their purpose the police would not hesitate to hang whatever crime on anyone at all.

Before I could even finish explaining to her what had happened, the Chamuca was already emptying the drawers of her desk of the things she was most attached to—a keyring made by the deaf and dumb, a paper-weight with a little flower inside it, and the like—and throwing them into her handbag.

The closest we came to being caught that day was when we went to pick up the Volkswagen. It was in the parking lot a block away from the Planning Office, where we always kept it. We had already entered the lot and were looking for the attendant when we saw him between the cars. He was talking with two men and the three of them were looking at the Volkswagen. That was enough for us. We left the parking lot without a word and got into a passing cab.

"Where are we going?" the Chamuca asked.

"To the Northern Bus Terminal," I told the driver.

I realized at this moment that I knew exactly what had to be done. The Chamuca looked at me blankly.

"You'll go to spend a few days with your cousin in Jerez," I told her.

"What about you?"

"I'm going to Muérdago to see my uncle Ramón and ask him for money."

Nobody in Mexico City knew the Chamuca had a cousin in Jerez or that I had a rich uncle in Muérdago.

"When I get hold of some money," I told the Chamuca, who was looking at me apprehensively, "I'll come for you and we'll go somewhere to live until this blows over."

She gave me her cousin's address and telephone number. I had never met her. We then scraped together what money we had between us. It amounted to 453 pesos, which was enough to cover the taxi, a first-class ticket to Jerez, a second-class ticket to Muérdago, and the stuffed pepper the Chamuca ordered in the terminal cafeteria and wasn't able to eat. We divided the rest, which came to sixty-one pesos each.

We then sat down inside the station to wait for the Chamuca's bus to be announced.

"What are you going to say to your cousin?" I asked.

"That I had a falling out with you. So when you phone me, it will be to beg my pardon, and when you come for me, it will be to make up."

I knew the Chamuca was very smart but sometimes I forgot.

"What about you?" she asked. "What do you plan to tell your uncle?"

"I haven't the slightest idea."

The worst moment of the day was when I caught sight of the Chamuca's face through the window of the bus as it was backing up to leave. She pushed the glass forward and I saw her crying, then the bus turned and she was gone. I stood facing the empty platform for a while and then I realized I was holding the Santa Marta poncho in my hand.

2

I will never forget my arrival in Muérdago. I stood at the corner of the arcade watching the people as they strolled round and round the square, listening to the serenade. I would have gladly changed places with any one of them. I felt tired, persecuted, and distraught. It had been a hard and nerve-wracking day, but at the moment it seemed tranquil in comparison to the ordeal of having to face an elderly uncle that very night who hardly knew me, was not expecting me, had no particular feeling about me, and had not even seen me in ten years, in order to tell him a story I had concocted on my way there.

It was ten minutes to eight by the clock on the church steeple. I was tempted to cross the street to the Universal Hotel, take a room, and go to sleep without thinking about the impending interview until the next morning. However, in consideration of the sixty-one pesos in my pocket and the fact that since I had no luggage I would certainly be asked to pay in advance, I desisted. Furthermore, I did not want to attract attention, and my beard and clothes were definitely conspicuous. Forcing myself to move on, I walked the length of the arcade, turned into Sonaja Street, and continued along it until I recognized my uncle Ramón Tarragona's house. My palms were sweating as I lifted the knocker.

The door was opened by a blond woman. We regarded each other in silence. Then I realized I had seen that painted red mouth before and the rather thick mole below it on her chin. She was the person I least expected and least wanted to see: Amalia Tarragona de Henry, my uncle Ramón's niece and my cousin by marriage.

"What do you want?" she asked, not recognizing me.

"I'm Marcos," I said.

She looked at my beard, Santa Marta poncho, and Argentine boots.

"Marcos who?"

She never did like me, inasmuch as she had always disapproved of anything associated with my dead aunt Leonor, but one might have thought she should have recognized me in spite of the beard, just as I recognized her with blond hair.

"Marcos . . . El Negro . . . your cousin."

"Marcos . . . Marcos González! A miracle! I haven't seen you in years. How you've changed! What are you doing around here?"

As she said these words, ostensibly an expression of welcome, I noted that she slipped her leg behind the door so that I wouldn't be able to push it further open.

"I want to see my uncle Ramón."

"What bad luck! You arrived just when he is having his supper and the doctor's orders are that nobody should interrupt his meals because it might disagree with him."

"I could stop by a little later."

"It would be even worse a little later because then he'll be asleep."

"How about my coming back tomorrow?"

"Frankly, I would advise you not to, because there's no telling what the emotion of seeing you might do to him. He's been in very delicate health, you know."

I was taken aback and did not know what to say next.

"You have no idea how sorry I am that I can't let you in. Ta, ta," she said, and shut the door.

I stood there for a moment, thoroughly disconcerted.

I set out along the dark street in the direction away from the square. I had to see my uncle now that I was in Muérdago, even if only to ask for money so I could move on. I decided to spend the night in the hotel and try again the next day. But I did not want to walk back to the square along the same street for fear of . . . yes, for fear of meeting up with Amalia again. I preferred to go all the way around the block.

It was fortunate that I did because, on rounding the second corner, I noticed a man wearing a hat who was locking the door of a pharmacy, and I recognized don Pepe Lara, a close friend of my uncle's.

"Don Pepe!" I said.

He looked at me for a moment and, seeing that I was about to say my name, he stopped me short with a gesture.

"Don't tell me who you are!"

He took me by the arms and made me do an about-face so that the light of the streetlamp shone directly on my face. He is a little, white-haired old man with round spectacles and a sharp nose who looks like an owl. He peered into my eyes for quite a while before speaking.

"You're Leonor's nephew. And your name is Marcos."

The two of us laughed. He embraced me and said, "Welcome to Muérdago!"

Then, backing off a step to take in the rest of me, he said, "Man, you look like the gaucho, Martín Fierro."

I felt more than ever that I had to get rid of my beard and change my clothes.

"How is it that Ramón didn't let me know you were in Muérdago?"

"I haven't seen my uncle yet."

I told him about going to my uncle's house and how Amalia had refused to let me in. He was not surprised.

"Amalia is a woman full of twisted notions whom

it is better not to cross," he said. "So let me make a suggestion. Stay here in my house overnight and, to-morrow, after she has gone to her shop, the two of us will pay Ramón a visit. You're going to be surprised at how glad he will be to see you and, when Amalia gets back, she won't dare turn you away again. How does that sound?"

It sounded fine to me. Don Pepe wanted to know if I had eaten supper, if I had any luggage, if I wanted to go to the Casino for drinks or would rather have them at his house. I chose the latter. He pushed open a door that was ajar next to the pharmacy, ushered me into a plant-filled vestibule, opened another door, turned on the light, and yelled, "Jacinta!"

It was a typical old-fashioned, small-town parlor with upright piano, Saltillo sarape on the wall, family por-trait, Purándiro lacquer bowl, and two china closets, one containing porcelain and clay figurines, and the other, bottles of liquor and glasses. Don Pepe removed his hat and hung it on the clothes rack. I realized that he wore it to go from his house to the pharmacy which was scarcely two meters away. He took a small key from his pocket, opened the closet where the bottles were, and turned to me.

"What do you prefer, Fundador or Martell?"

I preferred Martell. As don Pepe was pouring the drinks, a rheumatic woman wearing an apron over her black dress entered, stopped in the doorway of the par-lor when she saw me, and exclaimed, "Sweet Jesus, one thousand times."

"What's the matter with you?" don Pepe asked. "Don't you recognize him? It's Marcos, Leonor and Ramón's nephew."

"But he has a beard now," said doña Jacinta.

And—I said to myself—Argentine boots and a Santa Marta poncho.

"Beard or no beard," said don Pepe, "I recognized

him immediately because I looked at his eyes. They are exactly like his aunt Leonor's."

Doña Jacinta approached me with a timid smile and, holding her hand out to me, said, "Excuse me for not recognizing you, but the strange way people dress nowadays, you'd think they just came down out of the hills."

Her husband cut her short. "Marcos does not look like he just came down out of the hills. He looks like a modern young man." Considering the discussion closed, he went on to say, "Bring out olives and cheese and, besides whatever else you're serving for supper, fix a steak with potatoes, and then make up the bed in the guest room for Marcos. He is going to spend the night here."

After doña Jacinta had left the room, don Pepe and I sat down on a creaky old couch and he filled me in on what had happened with my uncle over the three years since his wife's death. He told me how, during the first year of his widowerhood, my uncle Ramón wore black, visited the cemetery frequently, bringing flowers, and gave up billiards as a manifestation of mourning. By the second year, however, he had taken to polishing off two bottles of mezcal a day, as he sat in the swivel chair of his office. One afternoon, Zenaida, my uncle Ramón's servant, came into the pharmacy and said to don Pepe, "The boss is on the ground and doesn't want to get up." Don Pepe found my uncle lying face down on the floor in his office, weeping into the carpet. "Ramón, what's the matter with you?" he asked. My uncle stopped crying and answered, "I've come to the conclusion that life without Leonor isn't worth living." Upset by this revelation, don Pepe consulted Dr. Canalejas shortly afterward as to whether my uncle might be capable of committing suicide, to which Dr. Canalejas replied that in his opinion my uncle was capable of anything.

However, my uncle Ramón did not commit suicide. He had a stroke. With one foot in the grave, he managed to survive. He left the hospital in a wheelchair, his left arm and leg paralyzed. Dr. Canalejas said that with a strict regimen and good care my uncle might live a year.

"Then," said don Pepe, " 'Handsome's' children came on the scene."

"Handsome's" children are the Tarragonas, my cousins, my uncle's brother's children. I am his wife Leonor's sister's son. My uncle Ramón and aunt Leonor were childless.

Don Pepe went on, "I am not insinuating that your cousins have acted calculatingly with an eye to the inheritance, but the truth is that, aside from yourself, they are the only apparent heirs. Ramón is the richest man in this town but they never paid the slightest attention to him until they found out that he had only a year to live. Now they've been hanging on every breath he draws since the day he left the hospital. Amalia and her daughter are living in Ramón's house so that they can look after him; Alfonso manages his business affairs; Fernando runs the hacienda; and Gerardo, who doesn't know how to do anything, comes to ask him how he's feeling every afternoon."

The year Dr. Canalejas gave him to live was up and he was still going strong.

"And now," don Pepe said, closing the subject, "tell me about yourself. Are you married?"

"No."

I had decided not to mention the Chamuca.

"How old are you?"

"Thirty-two."

"You are doing the right thing in not getting married. What's the rush? I didn't marry until I was forty. The last news I had of you was that you were studying mine engineering. Are you practicing your profession?"

"I am a mining consultant." With this statement I wiped out of my past the five years of boredom in the Planning Office.

"What does that consist of?"

"I have an office, and when a mining company needs an expert opinion about something, an exploration done, or a sampling made, they hire me. That's how I earn my living."

"Very interesting. I'm sure you'll make a success of it."

I was looking down at my Argentine boots. I decided not to exaggerate.

"Well, I'm just getting started."

"And what brings you back here after so many years?"

"I wanted to propose a business deal to my uncle but now I am wondering whether it would be a good idea, seeing that he is so ill."

"Tell me what the deal is and I'll tell you whether it's a good idea or not."

"Do you know what cryolite is?"

"Never even heard of it."

"It is the ore from which beryllium is obtained. Beryllium is a very important metal in industry. Its alloys are highly resistant to deformation produced by temperature changes and because of that it is in great demand. The price of beryllium has been going up recently because there is a world shortage."

"You don't say! Tell me more."

"I know where there is a cryolite deposit."

"And you want to sell it to Ramón."

"Not exactly. I want to offer it to him on a partnership basis. I tell him where the mine is, he puts up the money, I manage the mine and direct the operation, my uncle recovers his investment, and we split the profits."

"Sounds fair to me. What does the project involve?"

"It's relatively simple. There is an already existing mine. However, machinery has to be rented and the ore removed, loaded into trucks, and taken to Cuévano for processing. It is a small lode that will be exhausted in six months of production. That's why I don't make the offer to any of the big companies. They wouldn't be interested."

"Where is this mine?"

"I can't give you that information. It's all I have to sell."

"How much money will have to be invested?"

"A million pesos."

Don Pepe stood up and, looking at me very solemnly, said, "Young man, everything seems to indicate that what you have come to propose fits the bill to perfection. What's wrong with Ramón is not so much that he's ill but that he's being bored to death. A venture like the one you propose could be very beneficial for him. It's something different, something new and interesting for him to do, and not too risky. Whether he loses a million pesos or makes a couple of million doesn't much matter. What is urgent, though, is that he be distracted so he will stop thinking about his illness."

I ran through in my mind the story I had just told and was filled with admiration. With just a few lies I had justified my trip to Muérdago, as well as the bite I intended to put on my uncle. And not only that, but the beard, Santa Marta poncho, and Argentine boots had, all at once, taken on a certain respectability as the accoutrements of the man who combs the mountains in search of minerals.

Don Pepe threw his head back and peered at me from under his spectacles. "I should warn you," he said, "if Ramón takes an interest in your cryolite mine, 'Handsome's' children are going to detest you."

He seemed to be amused.

*   *   *

The bed made up for me by doña Jacinta was wide and comfortable, the sheets and pillowcases immaculate. Ensconced in it, I opened a book don Pepe had recommended to me, *The Medicinal Herb Garden*. The author was a Cuévano doctor of the early part of the century by the name of don Eustaquio Pantoja who, as don Pepe explained to me, devoted his life to collecting, classifying, and presenting in relatively clear terms the remedies of native Indian healers. I read of the uses of belladonna, what rue was good for, and, halfway through the description of cat's paw, I fell asleep. I dreamed I was in a huge airport in a strange city looking for the Chamuca without being able to find her. I woke up to the thunder of the church bells calling to Mass. Thin rays of sunshine entered through the slats of the shutters. The room was white. After a pleasurable moment, I remembered my situation.

Don Pepe and doña Jacinta were in the patio arguing. He, without a necktie and wearing an old jacket, was insisting that the bug she was on the point of squashing with the end of a broomstick was harmless, while she maintained that it was a centipede, an insect whose sting was mortal. As don Pepe was proving that it was impossible for it to be what she thought, doña Jacinta jabbed it with the broomstick, putting an end to the creature and the demonstration. Don Pepe grew red in the face but at the same moment, noticing me in the corridor, he turned to ask whether I had spent a comfortable night.

"I'd like to shave," I said. "Can you lend me a razor?"

The two of them looked at me with expressions of such approval that I understood they must have discussed my beard and decided that it was something I would be well rid of. Don Pepe said that he had an English straight razor with which he shaved himself for solemn occasions, such as his saint's day and Christmas Eve.

"Go and get it," he said to his wife. "It's in my wardrobe. Bring the bottle of toilet water, too."

While doña Jacinta was gone, I commented on how interesting I had found Dr. Pantoja's book.

"Keep it," don Pepe told me.

He then showed me some specimens he had growing in flowerpots. Pointing to a plant with tiny leaves and blue flowers, he said, "This one is *paxtle* or, as it is also known, old man's beard. It has remarkably versatile properties. Steeped as a tea it acts as a sleeping draught, crushed and inserted into the nostrils it alleviates the symptoms of the common cold, and as an infusion mixed with artemisia and taken during the day instead of drinking water, it will also induce abortion."

He had great faith in medicinal plants and complained about how so many of them have fallen into disuse.

"The doctors of today don't know how to use them," he said. "They prescribe patent medicines that are more expensive and, a good part of the time, less effective."

He added that Dr. Canalejas had put my uncle under treatment with a household remedy that was doing wonders for him.

Looking at my former face in the bathroom mirror, I felt younger, calmer, more innocent. When I walked into the dining room, shaven, my hosts applauded.

The sound of sparrows squabbling shrilly could be heard nearby. The Lenten cobalt sky hung over Muérdago. Visible on our left were the pink steeples of the church, two-story houses, and the laurel trees in the town square. The rest of the visual field encompassed the flat city of rooftops, relieved at intervals by a tower, a dome, and a solitary ash tree, and cultivated parcels stretched out all the way to the background of the mountains in the distance.

Don Pepe and I crouched, peeping through the potted geraniums. We had gone up to the roof of his house to have a look at my uncle's house, which was situated directly behind. Right below us were the chicken coops, further back the service patio, and in the rear we could make out a portion of the front patio and corridor. We wanted to be sure Amalia had left my uncle's house before we visited him. Don Pepe knew that every morning she went to attend to her women's-apparel shop, the name of which was Casa Amalia.

"It seems," said don Pepe, "that she stays in her store only long enough to see if there is anything to be taken care of and to collect the previous day's receipts, but that will give us enough time."

The chickens began to cackle, the little door of the henhouse opened, and a young woman entered, followed by a dog.

"That's Lucero," don Pepe said.

The daughter of Amalia and her husband "The Gringo," Lucero, a pallid little girl ten years ago, was now transformed into a beautiful woman. I observed her from my hiding-place behind the geraniums. She had light chestnut hair and golden-skinned arms, and she carried a pail filled with corn on her hip. Scooping out handfuls of the kernels, she threw them to the chickens, setting off a tremendous racket. Every once in a while, the dog would chase a chicken, which fled squawking in panic. Lucero's movements were gracefully deliberate.

When the corn was all gone, Lucero shook out the pail, slapping it against her hip, left the henhouse with the dog at her heels, and shut the door.

"How pretty she is!" I said.

"Yes, she is pretty," don Pepe replied, rummaging in his jacket pocket for his cigarettes.

We sat on the stone roof-ledge and smoked.

In a little while we heard the clicking of heels. Once again, we crouched behind the geraniums. We could see Amalia with an elaborate hairdo, dressed in purple, carrying a pink umbrella in her hand as she walked through the corridor of my uncle's house, followed by her daughter, a step behind.

"Your cousin," don Pepe commented, "is the only woman in the entire state of Plan de Abajo who uses an umbrella in the dry season."

As soon as we heard the big front door slam, we started down the steps.

My uncle, Ramón Tarragona, was seated in his wheel-chair in the corridor of his house reading *Excélsior*. Don Pepe and I were in the middle of the patio between the begonias and the elephant's ears. (The door had been opened by Zenaida, the old servant, who recognized me immediately and was overjoyed to see me.) "Eight Terrorists Arrested," said the headline on the front page of the newspaper my uncle was holding. When he heard our footsteps, he tilted the paper down, revealing his face. The right half was that of an old but sprightly, intelligent-looking man, while the left half had the appearance of a poorly rendered copy, devoid of expression. On that side, the only thing that seemed to have life was his eye, which was scrutinizing me over the top of his glasses.

"Guess who this is," said don Pepe.

I stood there with my Santa Marta poncho and the book by Dr. Pantoja in my hand, not knowing what to do. I wanted to read that newspaper, I wanted to see my uncle's face, and, at the same time, I wanted to have him recognize in my face the unmistakable stamp of the honest man: the level gaze of eyes that look straight ahead, with frankness, unblinking. It was my uncle's face that claimed my attention when his lips on the right side parted to expose purple gums and yellowish teeth. It took a moment for me to realize that he was smiling.

"It's Marcos," he said. His voice was the same as ever.

He dropped the newspaper when he raised his right hand.

"He wants to embrace you," don Pepe said in a low voice.

I went clumsily up the four steps that separated the patio from the corridor and gave my uncle Ramón the awkward embrace permitted by the newspaper lying between his legs and the floor, the wheelchair, the poncho in my hand, and Dr. Pantoja's book. I smelled of sweaty clothes, my uncle of imported soap. He wore tweed trousers, a vest, and a necktie.

"How are you?" it occurred to me to ask.

"Up shit creek, as you can see," he answered.

Don Pepe picked up the newspaper and put it on the little table.

"When did you arrive?" my uncle asked.

"He just got off the bus," said don Pepe.

We had agreed to say nothing about the night before.

"Pull up chairs," my uncle directed.

We obeyed and sat down. My uncle, continuing to give orders, addressed me. "Give an account of yourself. What have you been doing?"

I reeled off the same story I had told don Pepe the night before. Using only his right hand, my uncle pulled out of his vest pockets a cigarette holder that he put in his mouth, a Delicado that he inserted in the holder, and a lighter with which he lit it. He smoked as I spoke.

Don Pepe, who had taken off his hat, sat on the edge of a rocking chair, resting his hands on his knees and looking at me intently as though he were hearing for the first time what I was saying, and was anticipating an intensely engrossing account.

Again I said nothing about either the Chamuca or the Planning Office, but I did embellish the description of my invented profession with new details. I located my office on Palma Street and mentioned the names of three companies that had contracted my services. The interest with which my uncle followed my exposition and the favorable impression I was apparently making on him filled me with confidence.

He interrupted me to say, "Tell me, what brought you here?"

"I came to propose a business deal to you."

"Is that so? It better be a good one," my uncle said, lighting a fresh cigarette from the butt of the previous one. "What is it all about?"

"Do you know what cryolite is?"

"No."

"It's an ore that . . ."

"Don't tell me what it is, tell me what it has to do with the business deal."

"I know where there is cryolite."

"How much will it cost to extract?"

"One million pesos."

"After we've taken it out, how much can we get for it?"

"Between four and five million."

"How long will it take us to mine it?"

"Not more than six months."

"All right. I'm interested."

Don Pepe cut in, saying, "Don't be giving him an answer like that. Let him explain to us." And, turning to me, he asked, "How is cryolite mined?"

"In this case, very simply, because there is a gallery that leads to the lode. It is an abandoned mine."

"In the state of Plan de Abajo?" my uncle asked.

"Yes."

"So much the better. If there should be any problem about the permit, the governor will give us a hand. He's a friend of mine. I accept your proposition."

Like don Pepe, I felt that the agreement had been reached too quickly.

"I have to warn you, uncle," I said, "that before you put up the total investment it would be advisable to have a costs and profitability study made. It will include a topographical survey and a few assays to give us an approximate idea of how much exploitable ore there is, since the figures I am giving you are based on my visual impression."

"Sounds very sensible to me," said don Pepe.

My uncle waved his arm in a gesture of resignation. "Have the costs and profitability study made, then."

This was the moment I had been waiting for.

"The charge for that will be fifty thousand pesos," I said.

"If I can put up a million pesos, I guess I can manage fifty thousand."

"But," I warned him, "you'll have to pay me that amount even if the study should show that it is not an advisable investment."

My uncle hesitated a moment before speaking. "Agreed. But, if the study shows that it is, we go fifty-fifty. Right?"

I accepted. My uncle said, "Push me to my office and we'll draw up the contract right now."

I pushed the wheelchair with don Pepe guiding me. He opened the door to the office, a spacious, rather dark room the basic furnishings of which consisted of a rolltop desk and an old-fashioned cast-iron safe. There were also a bookcase that contained four volumes on agriculture and a copy of the constitution of the state of Plan de Abajo, several wooden filing cabinets, and a leather couch and two armchairs. We wrote out the contract by hand, don Pepe one copy and I the other. I was obligated to deliver samples of cryolite ore of no less than .08 metal content within five days of signature of the agreement. My uncle agreed to advance ten thousand pesos of my fee upon receipt of the results of the assay and proof that the mine we were going to exploit had no current prior claim entered in the Mine Registry. In the course of the subsequent ten days, I was to turn over the costs and profitability study, after which he would pay me forty thousand pesos regardless of the final decision. If the mine went into operation, I would be the manager, my uncle would recoup his investment, and we would divide the profits in equal shares. My uncle and I signed and then, as witnesses, don Pepe and Zenaida, who could not read or write but was able to sign her name and did not want to hear what was in the contract.

When Zenaida had left, my uncle twisted the knobs of the safe, opened it, and, instead of putting his copy of the contract inside, as I expected him to do, took out a bottle of mezcal and three glasses. My uncle laughed at my surprise.

Don Pepe explained, "Dr. Canalejas considers a drink every once in a while good for Ramón. Amalia, on the other hand, thinks alcohol is fatal for him."

"She doesn't let me smoke, either," added my uncle. He filled the glasses, using his good hand, and asked, "What is the name of this mine?"

"The Covadonga."

"To the Covadonga, then," said my uncle, raising his glass.

The three of us drank. At the same moment, the

creaking of a door being opened could be heard. Instantaneously the picture changed. My uncle and don Pepe gulped down the rest of their drinks, my uncle put the cigarette holder between his lips, pulled the cigarette out and before I had time to ask what was going on slipped it between my fingers, winking at me with his good eye, returned the holder to his vest pocket, and with a rapid movement tossed his copy of the contract into the safe.

"Put that away," he said to me, indicating my copy.

I folded it and shoved it into my shirt pocket. Don Pepe had meanwhile put the bottle and glasses back in the safe, shut the door, and, twirling the knobs, cleared the combination.

"Act like you've been talking," said my uncle.

We couldn't. The three of us just sat listening to the sound of Amalia's heels as she approached along the corridor. She stopped on the threshold and stood, blinking at us.

"Good afternoon. Who's here?"

She was carrying the pink umbrella, which had obviously not been opened. The purple dress accentuated the spectacular figure of a beauty of the days of President López Mateos: pear-shaped behind, narrow waist, and miraculously uplifted breasts. Her brown skin was darker than her dyed hair, and though she plucked her eyebrows, there were black hairs on her legs. She had magnificent, myopic eyes. Barely able to make out the three figures in the room, she wore a vaguely polite smile that showed her strong teeth.

"It's Marcos," said my uncle Ramón.

The smile vanished.

"Oh, hello there. It smells of cigarettes in here."

"Marcos and I have been smoking a lot," don Pepe lied.

My uncle cut her interruption short. "Marcos is going

to spend a few days with us. Have the twins' room made up for him."

Amalia threw me a look charged with ill will but smiled at my uncle, saying, "Of course." She turned and the three of us watched her as she walked away, a purple shape on legs that for some reason seemed provocative to me.

After don Pepe left and my uncle went off to his bedroom, I was alone. The first thing I did was to go to the little table in the corridor and open *Excélsior*. There were photographs on page 12 of all the people who had been at my house the night before last, except Pancho. Several of them looked like criminals, especially "Paws." Lidia Reynoso resembled a Spanish Civil War heroine. Ifigenia Trejo looked repentant. The story mentioned the party: We had met in my apartment "to hatch new plots." The seven had admitted that they were members of the "Gualterio Gómez Liberation Group" and confessed to having set fire to El Globo department store. Two members of the gang had managed to escape, but—the article reported—their capture by the Division of Investigation was imminent. Neither my name nor the Chamuca's appeared in the list nor, evidently, had the police given the newspapers photos of us, which they must have found in the apartment. Detectives had located the car abandoned by the fugitives in a parking lot on Edison Street.

I left the newspaper on the little table and went to the twins' room, which I knew was at the end of the corridor. On passing by the open door of Amalia's bedroom, I could hear her voice, saying, ". . . apparently he came to make some sort of business proposition . . ."

She was talking on the telephone, brushing vigorously at the same time with her hand at something on the front of her dress, over her breasts. She left the sentence hanging when she saw me. We looked at one another in silence for a moment before she pushed the door shut with her foot, and I continued on my way. I could hear her saying, "El Negro just passed by and overheard me. . . ."

3

The twins' room originally belonged to my uncle Ramón's twin sisters who died in their youth in 1920 in the same week, of the Spanish flu. It was kept intact and used as a guest room to accommodate occasional visitors. I was familiar with it myself, having spent two vacations as a boy visiting my uncle's house. It was a "feminine" room: pink wallpaper, light-blue spreads on the two beds, dark-blue rugs, and a water-color of a Pierrot on the wall. Everything was faded. One of the bedspreads had been removed and a woman was bending over the mattress unfolding a sheet. I could see her light-chestnut hair and smooth, tanned arms. It was Lucero.

She had not heard my footsteps, nor was she aware that I was on the threshold. She straightened up suddenly and with a quick movement threw her arms upward, making the sheet fly open. Both of us were startled, she at discovering she was not alone and I at the realization that I was in the presence of a fully formed woman. As the sheet floated down over the mattress, she regained her composure before I did mine and she said, "You're Marcos."

"You're Lucero."

"You taught me to play two-handed canasta."

"You were a skinny little girl crying with boredom in the corridor."

She studied me from head to toe.

"I would never have recognized you."

She disturbed me. I put the Santa Marta poncho and Dr. Pantoja's book on a chair.

"Nor I you."

"You were very handsome."

"You were horrible-looking."

She laughed and began tucking the ends of the sheet under the mattress. I went to the window and looked out at the ruin that used to be the stables.

"When was it?"

"Ten years ago."

"Do you think I am horrible-looking now?"

I looked at her and, after a moment, said, "No."

She laughed again and, without interrupting her bed-making, said, "I still remember the game you taught me. I play it sometimes, even yet."

"I've forgotten it. What are you doing now?"

"Making the bed."

"I mean, besides that. Do you go to school?"

"I play chess with my uncle."

"Why? I mean, why aren't you studying something?"

"Because I finished preparatory school, which is as far as one can go in Muérdago. I was supposed to enter medical school in Pedrones but my uncle took sick and my mother and I had to come here to look after him."

"That's a shame!"

"I don't mind. There's something else I do. I draw."

"What do you draw?"

"Faces. I draw people's portraits."

"What do you do with them when they are finished?"

"Throw them in the trash."

She wasn't wearing a brassière. I helped her extend the bedspread.

"How do you get along with my uncle?"

"Better than with anybody, and he loves me more than anybody."

I looked at her respectfully. The bed was made. At that moment Amalia entered.

"What are you doing here?" she asked Lucero.

"I came to make the bed."

"Zenaida should have made it."

"She was setting the table."

As I was considering what a difference there was between mother and daughter, Amalia turned to me. "Where is your luggage?"

"On that chair," I said, pointing to the Santa Marta poncho and Dr. Pantoja's book.

Amalia looked at them for a moment in disbelief but made no comment. All she said was, "My uncle is expecting us at the table."

She left the room, Lucero winked at me before following her out, and I brought up the rear.

The Tarragona dining table had always sat ten persons around it with room to spare. They say that when my uncle inherited it on the death of his parents, he objected to taking out the extra leaves. Most of the time for many years it was occupied by two people, my uncle Ramón at the head and my aunt Leonor on the side, next to him. That afternoon, the table, covered with a spotless white cloth, still seemed huge. My uncle looked like God the Father. He sat in his accustomed place, a white napkin held up by two clips covering his chest, his back to the amber-colored stained-glass windows. Two places had been set on his right and three on his left, the middle one of which was occupied by "The Gringo." "The Gringo" is Jim Henry, Amalia's husband and Lucero's father, a very tall man whose hair, parted on the side, always has a tuft standing up. He hadn't aged five minutes since I last saw him. He was wearing

the same lumberjack shirt. He seemed neither surprised nor pleased to see me, nor did he stretch out his
hand. He continued pulling the napkin out of his napkin ring and spread it over his knees.

"Hi," he said.

"Hi," I answered.

"Who is the sixth place for?" my uncle inquired.

"For my brother Alfonso," said Amalia. "He said he
would be coming for lunch."

"I wonder what he wants?"

"To say hello to you and see how you are, I guess."

"You're going to have to let Alfonso know that
whenever he wants to say hello to me and see how I
am, instead of notifying you that he is coming to lunch
he should ask me if I want to see him."

Amalia bit her lip and snapped at me with some
ferocity, "You sit over there!"

I had been about to sit down next to Lucero, on my
uncle's right. Amalia made me sit next to "The Gringo"
at the setting farthest from the head of the table. She
sat down between "The Gringo" and my uncle. Amalia
was the last to be seated, and just as she had accom-
modated her buttocks on the chair, Zenaida entered
with the white china tureen and set it on the table
beside her. Amalia dished out the soup in the following
order: my uncle, "The Gringo," Lucero, and me, last.
It wouldn't have taken much for her to have served
herself before me. "The Gringo," whose neck appears
to be riveted because he cannot turn his head without
swivelling his entire trunk, tried to launch into conversation with me.

"What's new in Cuévano?"

"I don't know. I left there eight years ago. I live in
Mexico City."

"I see. And what's new in Mexico City?"

And so on.

Lucero buttered a tortilla, rolled it into a little taco and handed it to my uncle, fixed another and gave it to "The Gringo," then a third and ate it herself. She didn't give me anything. We had noodle soup, which was served according to my aunt Leonor's custom, as I recall, each person adding chunks of fresh cheese and fried guajillo chili peppers to his taste. I was on my third spoonful when a man with bushy eyebrows and an extremely fine mustache entered. He was dressed to kill in an avocado-colored suit and a canary-yellow shirt. He raised his arms in a sign that we should not move, causing his cufflinks, massive wristwatch, and several rings, all of gold, to flash, saying at the same time, "Don't get up, don't disturb yourselves, just ignore me and keep right on eating."

It was my cousin Alfonso Tarragona, the banker, alias "The Golden Boy." He went to the head of the table and tried to kiss my uncle's good hand, but my uncle wouldn't let him and he had to be satisfied with picking up the lifeless one that was resting on the table and bringing it to his lips, after which he kissed Lucero, whose mouth was full, on the cheek, and greeted Amalia and "The Gringo" with a wave of his hand. It was not until this point that he appeared to notice my presence, feigning a paroxysm of pleasure at the sight of me. Walking all the way around the table, he came toward me with arms outstretched, and said, "Cousin! It's a treat to see you! What a terrific surprise!"

As I wiped my mouth with my napkin and stood up, I concluded that Alfonso was the person Amalia had telephoned to say that El Negro was in Muérdago. We greeted one another like generals: embrace, slaps on the back in the clinch, and handshake. He slipped into the seat beside Lucero and I went on eating my soup.

Alfonso asked my uncle, "How have you been doing?

How are you feeling? Have you had any new complaints?"

"I haven't been feeling any better or any worse than at other times."

"That's great!" said Alfonso and added, addressing the others, "Those old-timers have constitutions of iron. How I envy them!" Then, turning to me, he went on, "And you, Marcos, what fortunate winds have sent you our way?"

"A business trip," I said.

"Ah, I see, and you took advantage of it to drop in and pay your respects to uncle Ramón whom you haven't seen in . . . how long?"

"Ten years."

"Ten years! Imagine that! How time flies! So that means you weren't in Muérdago when aunt Leonor died?"

They had now promoted her. She used to be "my uncle's wife."

"No," I admitted.

"Or when my uncle took sick, either?"

"No."

"You must find things here very changed. In any case, I am delighted that it occurred to you to come and give us a chance to have a look at you again."

He swallowed a spoonful of soup, wiped his mustache with the napkin, and continued to interrogate me.

"Where did you leave your car?"

"I didn't drive. I came to Muérdago by bus."

"That's terrible! I certainly am sorry. What an uncomfortable trip that must have been!"

"The Gringo" now took the floor. "How come you didn't drive? Don't you have a car?"

The spoonful of soup on the way to Alfonso's mouth halted in mid-passage. Lucero stopped buttering the tortilla she was preparing for my uncle; Amalia and

"The Gringo" observed me closely; only my uncle went on eating unconcernedly.

"My car is in Mexico City being repaired. I had an accident."

"Sorry to hear that. What bad luck!"

"What make is it?" "The Gringo" asked.

"An International pickup truck," I lied, because I did not want to mention my Volkswagen, now in the hands of the Division of Investigation.

"Why a pickup truck?" Alfonso wanted to know. "Do you raise pigs, or what?"

"I am a mining consultant," I said.

The mention of this invented profession was met by a respectful silence that held for fifteen seconds.

"Don't you own any other vehicle?" asked "The Gringo."

I decided I was in no position to be inventing another car and another reason for not using it.

"No," I said.

"He has no luggage, either," Amalia added.

They looked at me in silence for a moment, and then Alfonso said, "Did you have to get out of Mexico City in a hurry?"

While I was considering how to answer, my uncle spoke, addressing me. "Your cousins, Marcos, are very interested in knowing why you came to Muérdago. Don't upset yourself trying to think up explanations. Tell them the truth. Tell them you came because I sent for you."

Everybody's attention, which had been focussed on me, now turned to my uncle, who was calmly stuffing into his mouth a ball of noodles too large for it and sucking them up noisily. I knew that the storm had blown over when I saw that the next taco being prepared by Lucero was for me.

"If you could use a shirt," "The Gringo" said, "I can lend you one."

"Thank you, but I don't need a shirt," I said, even though the one I had on was soaked.

"If you want to go anywhere," said Alfonso, "on business or just to roam around, don't go by bus. Come to the Banco de la Lonja, which is just out here on the corner, ask for the director, which is me, and you say to me, 'Alfonso, I want the car,' and I'll lend you my Galaxy right then and there."

When Zenaida brought in the main course, Amalia changed the order of serving and passed me my plateful right after my uncle received his. Later, when we got up from the table, as "The Gringo" lit a cigar and Alfonso and Lucero were pushing my uncle's wheelchair to the corridor, Amalia took me by the arm and, with a smile intended to be coquettish, said, "I assume you didn't tell my uncle that you arrived in Muérdago last night and that I wouldn't let you in when you came to the house."

"I didn't tell him and was not intending to."

"You're doing right. My uncle would get agitated and it could be bad for him. Besides, it was his fault that it happened because he didn't tell me he had sent for you and that you were due to arrive, and as you ought to know, he has given strict orders not to let anybody into the house except the family and his closest friends."

On reaching this point, Amalia realized that she had committed various errors and tried to patch them up.

"Naturally, you are one of the family, too, but . . ."

"Don't worry. I understand your situation."

As we went through the doorway arm in arm, we had to squeeze together somewhat and I could feel the pressure of her rump against my thigh. I don't know whether it was accidental or not. The part of my shirt that came into contact with her continued to smell of heliotrope.

Alfonso said goodbye, explaining that he had an appointment at four o'clock with a special emissary from the governor of the state.

He repeated his offer to lend me the Galaxy, and left. The rest of us went to our rooms to "have a little siesta." My uncle, pushed by Zenaida and Lucero, went into the main bedroom, the first one beyond his office, and the only one with a private bathroom; Amalia and "The Gringo" entered the next room off the corridor; the third was the blue room where Lucero slept; the fourth was the twins' room. I did not go in but instead headed for the bathroom directly opposite.

It was a huge bathroom with wainscoting of white tile. The toilet sat on a platform, the washbasin was easily four feet wide, and an entire family could have taken a bath in the tub at the same time. A pair of black lace panties hung from one of the shower handles. Judging from the size of the garment, I assumed it must be Amalia's. The door closed but could not be locked from inside because the bolt was broken.

Back in my room, I removed the contents of my shirt pocket—the sixty-one pesos and my copy of the contract with my uncle—and put them on the dresser, took off my Argentine boots, noticing a hole in one of my socks, and stretched out on the bed made by Lucero. The Chamuca came into my mind in two images: first, her tearful face at the window as the bus was leaving, and then, her naked body when she was removing the bedspread and did not want to make love for fear that Evodio would hear us. The caged cenzontle in the corridor sang, the church clock struck four, a hornet flew in through the open window and after making a tour of inspection flew out again, the clicking of Amalia's heels could be heard in the corridor and then the sound of the bathroom door opening and closing twice. A short time passed.

I don't know whether it was a barely audible sound that caused me to look at the door. I saw the doorknob turning slowly, the door opening, and then, through the crack, Amalia's blond hair followed by her black eyebrows. I shut my eyes. I could tell she had entered the room because I could hear the sound of her bare feet on the tiles. Then there was silence. I opened my eyelids slightly and between the lashes managed to see Amalia examine Dr. Pantoja's book and, not finding what she was looking for, put it down on my poncho, look around, and take a step toward the dresser. I moved, trying to simulate a sleeping person on the point of waking up. Amalia stopped, turned, and left the room. Then I heard her walking away, her heels clicking. As I pondered the significance of that strange visit, I fell asleep.

I awoke shortly after five, went out into the corridor and saw Amalia in the patio talking to two men. I recognized my other cousins, Gerardo, the judge, and Fernando, the farmer. Amalia was speaking too softly for me to hear her; Gerardo listened with arms crossed and bushy eyebrows frowning, Fernando caressed his mustache thoughtfully. I suspected from their expressions that Amalia was relating the incidents surrounding my arrival and what my uncle had said at the table. When Fernando saw me, he nudged Amalia with his elbow, waved to me, forcing a smile, while Gerardo, more demonstrative, stretched his arms toward me and said, "Cousin, give us a hug."

The two of them came out to meet me while their sister lagged behind adjusting her brassière straps. Gerardo is fat, gray-haired, and pink; Fernando, thin and ungainly. Gerardo wore a three-piece suit, Fernando, a windbreaker and denim pants. Gerardo hugged me tightly, Fernando gave me his fingertips to shake.

"Amalia tells us you are going to spend a few days in Muérdago. I think that's just great and so does Fernando. Don't you, Fernando?"

"Yes, I think it's great."

"I don't have to tell you, there isn't much to do in this town or much to see but, in any case, if you want to go somewhere, count on me, and on Fernando. Right, Fernando?"

"Yes, if you think I can be of any use, count on me."

"If you have nothing to do at any point and you get bored, come to the courthouse and we can have a chat or play dominoes. Fernando could run you out to the hacienda. Right, Fernando?"

"Yes, if you want, I'll take you."

"This is the melon season," said Amalia, who had come over to join us.

The sound of a ball smacking against a wall could be heard and two boys came running into the patio kicking a soccer ball and damaging the plants.

"My sons," said Gerardo proudly. "I bring them here frequently to say hello to uncle Ramón because he dotes on them. Right, Fernando?"

"Yes, he doesn't seem to mind them."

At that moment, my uncle, pushed by Zenaida and Lucero, appeared in the doorway of his bedroom. Seeing the soccer game in progress, he said, "Gerardo, tell those boys to go and play somewhere else."

"Say hello to your uncle Ramón, children, and then you can go home."

The boys went over to my uncle, kissed his good hand, and left without a word to anybody. As they were going out the front door, my uncle said to Lucero, "Bring the alcohol and a cloth to clean my hand."

Gerardo came over to me and explained in a low tone, "I feel it is very important for young people to be in contact with old age and to accustom themselves to it. Don't you agree with me, cousin?"

I agreed with him.

"Do you know what I feel like doing, boys?" said

my uncle as Lucero was wiping off the back of his hand.
"I feel like going to see the sunset from the top of
Rabbit Hill."

There was a moment of silence. It was obvious that
my cousins were not interested in seeing the sunset
from anywhere, but they recovered their composure
quickly.

"Sure! A great idea," said Gerardo. "Right, Fernando?"

"If that's what uncle wants, let's go."

"Yes, I do, and I want you to come too, Marcos,"
said my uncle.

The three of us lifted the wheelchair and carried it
down the four steps from the corridor to the entrance.
Gerardo's car was right there at the door. Lucero and
Zenaida, between them, passed my uncle from his
wheelchair to the front seat in what appeared to be a
simple maneuver. However, when we were on the hill-
top, we three men had to struggle till we were sweating
to move my uncle from the car seat back to the wheelchair.

"Push me over to there," my uncle said to Fernando,
pointing to the edge of the cliff.

My uncle gave my cousins perfunctory orders without ever bothering to say "please" and behaved in front
of them as if Amalia were there, that is to say, very
differently from the way he had acted with don Pepe
and me, never smoking or swearing. As Fernando and
my uncle moved off, Gerardo made a show of pulling
out his bandanna to mop his sweaty face, but actually
it was a pretext to speak to me alone.

"Amalia says my uncle asked you to come. How did
he communicate with you?"

I realized I had to go on lying.

"By mail," I answered. "He wrote me a letter." Even
as I spoke, the doubt entered my mind as to whether
my semi-paralyzed uncle would have been capable of

writing a complete letter. Gerardo's next question indicated that he was. "What did he say in his letter?"

"That he wanted to see me."

"What for?"

"He didn't say."

"Well, I imagine there must have been some reason for my uncle wanting to have you come now, after so many years of not seeing you. I wonder what's on his mind."

"You'll have to ask uncle, Gerardo. He is the one who can give you the answer."

"I know, but his answer will be that it's none of my concern."

"That's what I think, too."

We were both smiling. It was a good-humored confrontation.

"You're being unfair, cousin," Gerardo said, "because it does concern me. Tell me honestly, don't you think that the reason my uncle sent for you is connected with the inheritance?"

"What inheritance?"

"That uncle is going to leave his nephews."

"He hasn't mentioned anything to me about leaving me an inheritance," I said, which was the first truthful statement of the day. "Has he said anything to you?"

"Not explicitly." He looked at me out of his red, white, and green little eyes before making up his mind to talk frankly. "But it goes without saying. Let's take my brother Alfonso's case as an example. When uncle got sick, he said to Alfonso, 'Take charge of the portfolio.' The portfolio is uncle's stocks. There are a lot of them. Alfonso handles his investments, collects the dividends, turns over to uncle what he needs for his expenses, and reinvests the balance. Alfonso never tried to charge any commission for his work and my uncle never offered to pay him any. What would you gather from that? That if my uncle dies, God forbid, Alfonso will inherit the portfolio and that my uncle is letting him manage it now so he can gain experience. The same with Fernando. He lives on the hacienda, works from dawn to dark, keeps the books, and is responsible for the maintenance of the farm machinery. My uncle pays him the same wages the overseer gets: four thousand pesos a month. What does that mean? That he will inherit The Yoke. My sister Amalia's case: My uncle said to her, 'Come and live in my house with your daughter.' That's a nuisance for her, don't you think? 'The Gringo' sleeps home alone. It's logical that Amalia will inherit the Sonaja Street house when my uncle dies. As for myself, what is there to say? I manage his buildings in the San Antonio section. The people who live there are nothing but ruffians and you have no idea what I have to go through to collect the rent from them and, mind you, they are afraid of me because I'm a judge. The day my uncle dies, I am going to demolish those houses and sell the land, which is right on the highway, for putting up a factory or warehouses. Now do you get the picture?"

"Yes, it's perfectly clear."

"Then you don't get it. It's not clear at all. When my brothers and I made accounts, you weren't in the picture. That is why I am requesting, on behalf of my brothers and myself, that as soon as you know what he intends to leave you, you notify us so that we will have an idea of what is coming to us and be able to adjust our calculations accordingly. Don't you think the proper thing for us to do is to act like good cousins?"

"I agree," I said, and we shook hands with a smile, sealing the bargain.

Fernando had placed the wheelchair on a shelf of rock, from which my uncle commanded a perfect view of the landscape. The fertile lands of The Yoke were stretched out at his feet, bounded on one side by eroded hills and on the other by grubby little parcels.

". . . After you harvest those lentils," my uncle was saying to Fernando, "plant sorghum over there, and when the melon season is over, clear the ground and plant alfalfa."

"If you think that's what should be done, that's what I'll do," his nephew replied.

My uncle turned to me. It was obvious that the sight of his land rejuvenated him.

"What do you think of it, Marcos? Like an emerald in a garbage dump, isn't it?"

I looked at the wheat, which was beginning to gleam with a silvery light, the sorghum field, reddish and neatly groomed, the strawberry patches, and so forth. The drone of several tractors reached our ears.

"It's in splendid shape."

"This fellow here," said my uncle, pointing to Fernando, "is running the hacienda, and he hasn't done a bad job. The harvests are no better than when I was in charge, but they are not any worse, which is saying a good deal."

"I don't deserve any credit," said Fernando. "You plant, you water, and you bring in the crops. That's all there is to it."

Gerardo cut in to explain to me, "Fernando says that when he came to The Yoke, it was in such good hands and in such great shape that it was impossible to make a mistake."

"It's never impossible to make a mistake," my uncle said.

We regarded the field in silence for a while, and then my uncle pointed into the distance and reminisced. "I planted those eucalyptuses you see there myself, thirty years ago."

We kept on looking at the eucalyptus trees until my uncle pointed in another direction.

"And those ashes over there . . . I planted them forty years ago."

We looked at the ash trees until my uncle pointed into the sky.

"See that buzzard?" he said.

We watched the buzzard until my uncle said, "It occurs to me, Marcos, that Alfonso's Galaxy would not be the appropriate car for the trip you have to make tomorrow. I think Fernando had better lend you his Land Rover, since the road you will have to use is pretty rough."

I had no idea what "pretty rough" road I was supposed to travel on tomorrow because I had made no arrangements with my uncle about going anywhere. He looked at me very seriously, without blinking an eye. My cousins exchanged glances.

"What road are you referring to?" asked Gerardo.

My uncle answered immediately. "One that leads to the place where Marcos and I are going to set up a business."

Gerardo turned in my direction, expecting clarification. Fernando, however, gave up and said to my uncle, "It's your Land Rover and you can do whatever you please with it. If you consider that Marcos needs it to go somewhere, that's up to you. I'll have it outside your door by eight o'clock."

"Does eight o'clock suit you?" my uncle asked.

"Any time that's convenient for Fernando is fine with me," I said.

"All right, then, eight o'clock it is," said my uncle, concluding the conversation. "Let's go to the Casino and play poker."

"If you like, let's go to the Casino," said Fernando, who began pushing the wheelchair to the car.

Gerardo and I hung back again.

"What business are you going into with my uncle?" he asked.

"Better not ask me, because I'm not at liberty to say.

I gave my uncle my word of honor that I wouldn't talk about it. Why don't you ask him yourself?"

"He'll say it's none of my affair."

"He's probably right."

"Why do you treat me like that, cousin?"

Paco of the Casino, a short Spaniard who is the manager, came out to the lobby and received my uncle as though he were the owner of the place. He had one of the employees open the little room on the mezzanine that my uncle liked, went for the ivory poker chips he kept in the safe, and came back to the room a number of times during the course of the game to inquire if there was anything we wanted. My uncle drank nothing but mineral water, did not smoke, used no coarse language, and won all the hands but one. I underwent some anxiety because the initial stake amounted to two hundred pesos' worth of chips and all I had in my pocket was sixty-one pesos.

My uncle told a joke. He said that the situation he was in reminded him of the following story: "Johnny is at school in his zoology class and the teacher is explaining the habits of the hyena. 'The hyena,' she says, 'lives in the wilderness, eats rotten meat, cohabits once a year, and laughs. Is that clear? Are there any questions?' Johnny raises his hand and says, 'What I don't understand, teacher, is if the hyena lives in the wilderness, eats rotten meat, and cohabits once a year, why does he laugh?'"

We all laughed, especially Gerardo, who nearly choked.

"Just like me," said my uncle. "What am I laughing at?"

Fernando shuffled the cards and dealt.

"Is a straight better than three of a kind?" I asked. The three of them agreed that it was, but a short time later, when my uncle held three of a kind and I had a straight, three of a kind beat a straight, and my uncle raked in the pot.

Seeing that I looked disgruntled, Gerardo explained that three of a kind beat a straight in seven-card stud, which had been the dealer's choice that time around.

In another deal, Gerardo dropped out with two pairs, queens and fours, leaving two cards closed. My uncle won with three of a kind.

I was down to my last few chips when I picked up a flush. I stood pat and bet all my remaining chips plus fifty pesos from my pocket. After grumbling a bit, my two cousins dropped out. My uncle paid to see. He turned red in the face when he saw the five hearts I spread out.

"Good hand," he said, putting down two pairs.

Neither Fernando nor Gerardo dared say that two pairs beat a flush. I picked up the chips. At the same moment, my uncle said, "I'm tired. Let's go."

After taking out my fifty pesos, I had just enough to pay back the stack of chips I had received from the bank at the start of the game. Nobody noticed that I had been playing without money, which would have been shocking, I suppose, at least to my cousins. My uncle won 450 pesos, which he stuffed into his vest pocket. Gerardo lost the draw to decide who would pick up the check for the drinks. He paid and we got up from the table.

My uncle and I had supper in the dining room consisting of sweet rolls with coffee and hot milk. Amalia waited on us. Lucero had gone out and Zenaida was washing the kitchen floor. When we finished, my uncle wiped his mouth with his napkin and said to Amalia, "I want to talk to Marcos alone in my office. Bring a bottle of cognac and a snifter for him and a bottle of mineral water and a glass for me."

I rolled my uncle to the office and sat down opposite him on one of the leather armchairs.

"Don't feel that you are under any obligation to go somewhere tomorrow," he said. "I asked Fernando for the Land Rover just to annoy your cousins. I am sure they won't be able to sleep all night trying to figure out what possible business the two of us could be going into." He laughed gleefully at the thought of all the insomnia his joke was going to produce.

"As long as you got the car, I might as well use it," I said to him. "I'll bring you the samples tomorrow."

Amalia came in carrying a tray with a bottle of Martell, a bottle of Tehuacán water, a snifter, and a tumbler, and set it down on the little table.

"You should be aware, Marcos," Amalia said to me with great solemnity, "that my uncle is forbidden to smoke or drink."

"Shut the door as you leave," said my uncle.

When Amalia was gone, my uncle opened the safe, took out one of the shotglasses we had used in the afternoon for mezcal, made a sign to me to fill it, and tossed it off at a gulp without even allowing time to say "Salud." He sighed with satisfaction and made the same sign to me again. I refilled his glass.

"I'm going to ask a favor of you," my uncle said. "Every night for as long as you are in this house, I want you to drink Martell cognac, which is what I enjoy after supper, and smoke Delicados, my favorite brand. That way, the women will think it's you who is doing all the drinking and smoking. Get me? I want you to be my front."

"I'll be glad to do it, uncle," I said.

Later on, when Amalia came in to collect the glasses, I saw her eyes linger on the half-empty bottle of cognac and the eight cigarette stubs in the ashtray, but she made no comment.

4

I slept poorly. It was hot and I stripped, removed the covers, leaving only the sheet, and opened the window, letting in mosquitoes; Amalia, whom I imagined wearing a burnt-orange wrapper and high-heeled mules with marabou feathers, woke me up each of the four times she went to the bathroom; the church bells rang out every quarter-hour; awake, I worried about how the Chamuca was faring, asleep, I dreamed she had been run over by a moving van; at five A.M. the cenzontle was singing, at six the bells began to toll for early Mass and the sparrows began to bicker. I decided I must speak to the Chamuca that same day. At seven I got out of bed, put on my trousers, picked up the towel Lucero had hung over the back of a chair, and went to the bathroom. Amalia's panties were still dangling from the shower handle. I hung them on a hook on the wall and showered. Later, when I opened the door to my room, there was Lucero inside.

I stopped at the threshold in surprise. She was wearing a demure cotton robe in the style of elegant young ladies of a bygone era. She looked at me, flustered, one hand resting on the back of the chair on which I had put my shirt. All at once, she smiled.

"Close the door," she said.

I closed the door.

"I came to give you a kiss."

She walked over to me—I was holding the wet towel in my hand—put her arms around me, and gave me the most perfect kiss, technically speaking, that I had ever had in my life. I dropped the towel and tried to pull her robe off. Her body was delightful to touch but she defended herself with unexpected strength and determination, finally separating herself from me with a push, saying, "That's all!"

She left the room. Not yet fully comprehending what had happened, I turned toward the twins' dresser and looked at myself in the mirror. I saw a man with his mouth open, naked to the waist, his trousers misshapen with the bulge of an erection.

A little later, when I was putting on my shirt, I noticed that the sixty-one pesos and the copy of the contract that were in the pocket had changed places.

My uncle was dunking a sweet bun in his cup of chocolate when I entered the dining room. He winked at me in reply to my good morning. Amalia stood beside him counting the drops she was squeezing out of a medicine dropper into a glass of water. The bathrobe she wore, which I had pictured as being burnt-orange, was actually a yellow that made the dark tones of her skin look more pronounced—and her blond hair more ridiculous. She replaced the dropper in its bottle and smiled at me amiably.

"What kind of a night did you have?"

"Fine," I answered.

"I'll bet you got no sleep," said my uncle, biting into the bun and adding with his mouth full, "Nobody ever sleeps well in this house the first night."

He swallowed the last of his chocolate, wiped his mouth with his napkin, picked up the glass with the medicine Amalia had prepared, drained it, replaced the glass on the table, and belched.

"This medicine," he explained, "tasted foul when I first began taking it, but I've gotten used to it and now it has no taste at all."

"What is it?" I asked.

"Zafia water," said Amalia. "It has done him a world of good. What would you like for breakfast?"

I told her what I wanted and she left the dining room carrying with her a little violet-blue glass bottle with a label on which I was able to make out the words "Farmacia La Fe," the name of don Pepe Lara's drugstore.

"The Land Rover is outside, as agreed," said my uncle, taking a key from his vest pocket, putting it on the tablecloth, and shooting it in my direction with a strong and fairly accurate snap of his thumb and forefinger. "The tank is full."

I picked up the key, relieved to know that I would not have to spend my sixty-one pesos on gasoline.

My uncle said, "One of the hacienda tractor drivers brought the Land Rover and left it in front of the house, ate a taco Zenaida gave him, and went back to The Yoke on foot."

I was aware that it was a two-hour walk.

"I'm grateful to the tractor driver for his trouble and also to Fernando."

"The Land Rover belongs to me and I pay the tractor driver's salary," said my uncle.

"In that case, it's you I am grateful to."

"Don't be a horse's ass! Do you need anything?"

I thought a moment before I said, "A flashlight, a hammer, and a chisel."

"Ask Zenaida for them."

He reached into another pocket of his vest, took out a bill which he folded into four, put it on the tablecloth, and with another snap of his fingers shot it over to where I sat. It was a thousand-peso note.

"It's an advance against your fee," he said to me, "so you won't have a hard time."

"Why should I have a hard time?"

"Lucero went through your clothes and tells me that all you have is sixty-one pesos."

Since changing a thousand-peso bill can sometimes present a problem, I decided to walk over to the Banco de la Lonja to do it. It is an old building on the corner of Sonaja Street and the town square, half a block from my uncle's house. I got into a line at one of the windows with three people ahead of me and waited my turn. Less than a minute went by before somebody with a grip like a pair of ice tongs took hold of my arm. It was Alfonso.

"What in the world is a person doing standing in line in this bank when he has influence here? Come with me."

We went through a little door in the counter, crossed the administrative area, and entered Alfonso's private office. Two color photographs of the same size hung on the wall. They were heavily retouched portraits of the governor of the state and of the President of Mexico.

"If Mr. President were to visit this humble institution," he said to me, seeing that I was eyeing the pictures, "I would hang up a larger one I have of him. Meanwhile, I leave them as they are because the governor comes here all the time."

He had me sit in a narrow armchair and himself sat in a wider one behind his desk, which stood on lion's claws.

"What can I do for you, Marcos?"

"All I wanted was to change a bill."

I handed it to him. He unfolded it, studied it, opened a drawer, checked it against a list he took out, seemed satisfied, put the list back, and shouted, "Elenita!"

A dark-skinned woman with very red lips and mar-
celled hair, wearing a spectacular dress, entered.

"Elenita, this is my cousin Marcos González . . .
señorita Elenita Céspedes, my private secretary."

"Pleased to meet you," Elenita and I said simultaneously.

"My cousin would like to change this thousand-peso
bill, Elenita." He handed her the note and asked me,
"How do you want it, cousin?"

"Eight hundred in hundreds and the rest in tens," I
said, looking at Elenita.

"Eight hundred in hundreds and the rest in tens,"
Alfonso said to Elenita, as though she had not heard
me.

"Certainly, *licenciado*," Elenita said to Alfonso, and
left.

"I like to be surrounded by beautiful things," Alfonso said.

It took a moment for it to sink in that he was referring to Elenita. He went on, "I saw Fernando's car
in front of my uncle's house, which leads me to think
that the offer I made yesterday to lend you my Galaxy
is being snubbed."

"The thing is that I am going to be driving on a very
bad road and my uncle and I thought it might damage
your car."

"I'm not asking for any explanations, I just wanted
to point out two things: number one, that the offer still
holds, and number two, that I believe you made a poor
choice, because that tin can of Fernando's is not to be
compared with a Galaxy which practically drives itself."

Elenita returned, gave Alfonso the bills, and went
out again. Alfonso handed them over to me and said,
"My uncle gave you that thousand-peso note, right?"

"Yes."

"I was able to tell from the serial number." He paused,

I shifted uncomfortably in my seat, and he went on. "Don't feel under any obligation to tell me why he gave it to you. I just made the comment so that you would know I am keeping tabs on your affairs."

We took leave of one another with feigned cordiality, and I left the bank regretting that I had ever gone in. I walked to where the Land Rover was parked, climbed in, and after finally getting it started, took a little time driving about the streets of Muérdago until I found the way out to the Cuévano highway.

The highway runs downhill between mesquite trees, curves sharply, narrows to form a bridge leading out of the ravine, and then climbs the next hill. This sector is, or used to be, called "Los García." Why, I don't know. The junction of the roads is at the top of the second slope.

THE CAULDRON
DE LUXE ROOMS
INTERNATIONAL CUISINE
HOT SPRINGS
A TREAT! (10 KM.)

said the sign, which was new. The dirt road was un-changed. Leaving the paved highway at almost right angles, it climbs the slope hopping between the gar-ambullo trees. Neither the owners of the hotel nor the people who used to live in the settlement had put a hand to it in ten years; or, more likely, not in twenty. The car was shaken up, if not by stones slamming into it that it dislodged from the road, then by plummeting into craters camouflaged with fine dust. After travel-ling some three hundred meters along the detour, I could see in the trembling mirror that a small white car had come to a stop at the junction. I continued on my way without changing speed.

When I reached the top of the hill, I stopped the car

and, with the same strange feeling that comes over me every time I return to this place, I looked at the view that stretched out before me: four identical hills, like two pairs of breasts joined together, leaving a pan-shaped valley in the center called The Cauldron. Located at the foot of one of the hills are the famous springs from which the hot mineral waters pour into the spa and the plantations of sugar cane that constitute the region's only riches.

What a strange place to have been born in, I thought, as I do every time I return. I come from up in the hills, my dad was a loser, everybody calls me El Negro, life has handed me a screwing.

I started the Land Rover and moved forward in low gear. Again, I saw in the mirror that the small white car had left the highway, turned onto the detour, travelled along it for some distance, and stopped, just as I had done. A few meters ahead, the road curved around the hill, and I lost sight of the car.

"Nothing here but brush and cactus, except for the stones," as my father used to say, according to my mother. And so one day he told her he was going to Pedrones to buy pipe for the pump and we never saw him again. He abandoned my mother, a woman who loved him madly, and me, when I was a boy of seven.

I reached the bottom of the ravine where the drain overflows, producing a permanent bog and breeding-place for mosquitoes. I skirted the mud carefully without being concerned, however, about leaving tracks, and instead of proceeding along the road that leads to the white hotel buildings and the dun-colored ones of the settlement, I took the fork on the left, even more neglected, if possible, which winds around two of the hills and ends in a small valley formed by the conjunction of the other two. On reaching that point, I stopped the car, turned off the motor, and got out.

Everything looked the same: the Spaniard's house in ruins, the four eucalyptus trees still standing, the rusty rails sticking out of the tunnel entrance, and even the overturned dump car in apparently the same position as the last time I had visited the place, ten years ago, or the time before that, twenty-two years ago. We kids who played inside the tunnel used to call it "the old mine." Afterwards, I learned that its name was the Covadonga.

Taking the flashlight Zenaida had lent me and leaving the hammer and chisel in the trunk, I crossed the little valley to the tunnel and stopped at the opening. It was a black and forbidding hole, two meters wide by two high, that dampened any desire to enter. When I heard the sound of a car approaching, I mastered my feeling of repulsion, turned on the flashlight, and began walking through the tunnel. The odor of bat urine was just the same as it was when I went into the mine as a boy. The bats began to squeak and flutter as I advanced. The gallery seemed to be in good condition, the timbers sturdy, the walls and ceiling almost dry. I counted off fifty-two paces until I arrived at the point where the gallery becomes so low that I would have had to squat or crawl if I wanted to go on. Satisfied with what I saw, I turned back toward the entrance. Outside, the sound of a furiously racing motor could be heard. A car, evidently being driven recklessly, suddenly stopped. I continued walking, hugging the wall, until I reached the mouth of the tunnel, where I looked out through a space between the timbers of the first frame. The small white car had made a complete turn and was parked next to the Land Rover, ready to speed off. At that moment the door of the car opened and a man stepped out. It was "The Gringo" in his red and green lumberjack shirt. His gaze, travelling slowly, took in the ruined house, the eucalyptus trees, some piles of waste from the mine, the dump car, and the rails, and stopped at the tunnel mouth. We looked each other in the eye without his realizing it. He then got back into the car and drove off, leaving a cloud of dust behind.

I decided to kill some time. When the car was no longer in sight I came out of the mine, crossed the little valley, and went over to a stone bench alongside the door of the Spaniard's house, where I sat in the shade provided by some sheets of metal. I noticed no papers or empty cans among the yellow clumps of grass, nor any other signs of recent occupation. There were, however, many tracks left by the frequent passage of herds of goats. I looked at the hill in front of me, covered with huisaches, green because they were budding, and ash-colored garambullos, remembering that it is called The Hill Without a Name, which seemed to me an idiotic name for a hill. The sun was hot, not a leaf stirred, the sky was blue, a ring-tailed dove cooed. I decided that this melancholy song was a signal for me to be on my way.

Everything at the settlement was the same. A pack of skinny, vicious dogs chased the car, snapping at the wheels, some pot-bellied children threw stones at me, the houses were hidden behind the cactus grove. I recognized El Colorado's house by the lemon tree and the little gate. A man was seated on a small chair shucking corn. Five dogs received me at the entrance. On seeing that I was getting out of the car, the man stopped his work, stood up, crossed the corral, and kicked a white dog, the fiercest of them. I realized that he hadn't recognized me.

"I'm El Negro."

A smile nearly split his face into pieces. He looked at me, then at the Land Rover, and finally we shook hands.

"I can't believe it—Negro! Couldn't tell it was you, you've changed so much."

It was the same with me. I had never noticed before that besides being red-faced, El Colorado was also pock-marked.

"Let's walk," I said to him. "I want to talk to you."

He secured the door of his house with a piece of rope and we started off, he in front, I behind him. He didn't ask where I wanted to go because he already knew. We took the same walk we always did whenever I came back. We followed the old path that curves around by-passing the spa, climbs a steep slope, goes through the portal between the hills, crosses through the middle of The Cauldron where the huisaches are thickest, and ends at a spring called The Boiler. Nobody has ever seen the bottom of this hole ten meters in diameter because the steam that rises from its depths burns your face if you come close. The noise made by The Boiler is unforgettable. It is as though a giant were belching every three seconds, unremittingly, and the stench is equally foul. The spring empties into a narrow, winding canyon, leaving a vapor trail, until a point where the ground flattens and the water comes close to the sur-face. From there it is diverted into a pool for cooling, then into the bath-house, and finally to the cane fields. We stopped at the edge of the hole, where the ground was slippery but the steam did not bother us, and El Colorado asked the ritual question: "Remember Nate, the drunk, who got down right here on all fours and fell into the hole? We never saw him again. His hat was all The Boiler gave back."

"Yes, I remember," I said to him. "Do the women still come here when they want to boil a chicken, and throw it all plucked into The Boiler, tied to a cord?"

"They still do," said El Colorado.

After this conversation we began walking again, he in front, I behind. We followed the canyon till we came to the pool, stopping at the chalky mud where El Colorado asked me the other ritual question: "Do you remember when we used to go swimming here as kids and the time we were making such a racket that the lady who owned the place sent the attendant to chase us but we heaved stones at him and chased him."

"I remember," I said.

We started walking again. Entering the hotel by the rear door, we went through the hall and the empty yard until we came to the porch where there was a sign in English saying LADIES BAR. We sat down there at a table. Evidently the new owners had tried to turn The Cauldron into a tourist paradise and failed. Not only weren't there any customers, but nobody was behind the bar. A little later we heard the slapping sound of sandalled feet coming toward us through the corridor and a fat old woman in a very loose dress appeared; she had just washed her hair and had it draped over a towel across her shoulders.

"Doña Petra. She runs the place," El Colorado explained.

"What would you like?" doña Petra asked.

"A couple of beers," I said.

"If you'd do me the small favor," she said, "of taking them out of the icebox yourselves, because I just washed my hair in hot water and I might catch a chill if I put my hands into the cold."

After El Colorado brought the beer and we had taken a swallow, I said, "I'm trying to arrange a deal to operate the old mine."

"That's good," he said.

"Except there's somebody trying to scuttle the whole thing."

"That's bad."

"I need someone to be around day and night for the next two weeks who will see to it that nobody gets into the mine or, what would be worse, takes out any ore. Do you know somebody trustworthy who might be willing to take on the job?"

"Me. I've got two weeks to spare. My fields are cleared and I don't have anything pending until the rains start."

"Do you still have your carbine?" I asked.

"Still do."

"How much will you charge?"

"Whatever you'll pay."

"A hundred pesos a day."

"Fine."

I handed him two hundred-peso notes.

"An advance," I said.

"Good," he said, pocketing the bills.

We had to go to the office to pay doña Petra for the beer. There was a booth at one side of the counter that said "Long Distance." I was on the point of putting through a call to the Chamuca but changed my mind at the last moment. I had decided to use a false name— Angel Valdés—and El Colorado, who knew my real name, was standing beside me. I paid the check and we left.

In Cuévano, I parked the Land Rover in Constitution Square in front of the Mine Registry, bought copies of each of the five newspapers that had just arrived from Mexico City, and, carrying them under my arm, went into the Flor de Cuévano.

I ordered a cup of coffee and checked through the papers carefully. The news about the captured "terror-ists" that had appeared on the front page the day before was now relegated in *Excélsior* to page 18, and none of the other newspapers carried a followup story. The re-port in *Excélsior* was a rehash of what had come out the day before, except that the names of the fugitives were given, that is to say, their aliases, "El Negro," and "La Chamaca." There were no photos of us. The situation, I decided, was as favorable as might be expected under the circumstances.

Feeling calmer, I took out my address book to look up the Chamuca's cousin's telephone number, and the first thing that caught my eye was the note "Paws" had written in it that said, *Take launch that runs from port of Ticomán to Half Moon Beach (Aurora Hotel).* I interpreted this as a good omen and decided that it would be the ideal place for the Chamuca and me to hide out as soon as I got my hands on enough money. I went to the desk and gave the operator the number in Jerez.

"Who do you want to talk to?"

"Carmen Medina," which is the Chamuca's name.

"Who is calling?"

"Angel Valdés."

When the operator gave me the sign, I went into the booth and heard the Chamuca's voice asking suspiciously, "Yes?"

"It's Marcos."

I heard a mixture of laugh, sob, and incoherent speech.

"How are you?"

"I want to see you."

"But are you all right?"

"Yes, but I want to see you."

"Listen to me: tomorrow or the day after, my uncle is going to give me nine thousand pesos."

"What did you tell him?"

"Let me finish. If you feel you are in any danger or you don't like it in Jerez, tell me now and I'll come for you as soon as I have the money."

"Come for me."

"Let me finish. If you are not in danger and not unhappy there, and you can wait ten days more, it would be better because my uncle has to turn over forty thousand pesos to me and then I'll come for you and we'll be able to spend some time at Half Moon Beach, where 'Paws' stayed. Do you remember what he told us about it?"

"All right. I'll wait ten days more, then you'll come for me and we'll go to Half Moon Beach."

"Perfect! I'll phone you every chance I get."

"Tell me what you did to get so much money out of your uncle."

"I'm doing a study for an investment he is going to decide isn't advisable for him to make but which he is going to pay me for anyway."

She laughed, I said goodbye and hung up.

When I left the Flor de Cuévano, I crossed Constitution Square and threw all the newspapers I had bought into a trash can, after which I went along Triumph of Bustos Street until I came to a door that had a sign on it saying La Cueva de Ali Baba, and entered. It was an antiquarian's shop. In the dimly lit room I saw, heaped up in disorder, old books, votive paintings, termite-infested furniture, rusty locks, cloudy mirrors, and so on. A man was varnishing a chair. He straightened up when he saw me, and asked, "What are you looking for?"

"Cryolite."

He took me into an inner courtyard where there were old tools and piles of different kinds of rocks, all decorative, of the sort used by people for mineral collections or as doorstops. Knowing what I was looking for, I went directly to one of the piles and selected six specimens that seemed first-rate to me. Cryolite is a dense white stone with red veins.

"They are twenty pesos apiece," the man said.

I paid him and he gave me an old cement-bag in which to carry them. I took the bag out to the Land Rover and put it in the trunk. I then went to the Mine

Registry, where I purchased a 1:50,000-scale aerial map that showed The Cauldron and filled in an application for a "nonregistration certificate" for a mine by the name of the Covadonga in the municipality of Las Tuzas. Having done this, I went into a shop called El Caballero Elegante and bought two shirts and four pairs of socks. After leaving the shop, I was about to cross Constitution Square to pick up the Land Rover when I came to a very odd decision. I went into Dr. Ballesteros's drugstore and bought half a dozen condoms.

The small white car was on Sonaja Street outside my uncle's house. In parking the Land Rover I gave it a bump that was not entirely unintentional. It was after four o'clock. Zenaida opened the front door and helped me remove the things I had in the car.

"The boss left orders," Zenaida said, "that before you took your siesta I should give you whatever you wanted to eat or drink. So tell me what I can get you, young man."

I told her what I wanted and we went into the house together. We parted company at the entrance, she going toward the service patio with the tools she had lent me in the morning and I to the corridor with the cement-bag of rocks and the package from El Caballero Elegante. I tried to walk as quietly as possible because the bedroom doors were open. It was very warm. My uncle Ramón was asleep in the big iron bed practically in a sitting position, propped up with pillows. Amalia and "The Gringo" were lying in the twin beds, on their backs, arms pressed to their sides, legs out straight, stocking feet at right angles. They looked like the corpses of two who had died while standing at attention. Lucero was lying on her bed reading a book. She had glasses on. I was able to make out the title of the book: *La Casa Verde*. I stopped at her door. She looked at me over her glasses and smiled.

"Hi," she said.

"I want another kiss," I said.

"Not now," she said, and went back to her reading.

I walked on to the twins' room, put the bag of rocks on the floor and the package from El Caballero Elegante on the bed, took the aerial map out of my pocket, got my towel, and went to the bathroom. I took a long time. When I returned to my room, I found what I had expected. The bag of rocks had been moved slightly. Also, now, only five of the six rocks I had bought were there. I took the aerial map from my trouser pocket and put it in one of the dresser drawers, which were all empty, and covered it with my new shirts and socks. I went out to the corridor.

Lucero was still reading in her room. "The Gringo" had gotten up and was seated in one of the leather chairs in the corridor lighting a cigar.

"Hi," he said on seeing me. "We missed you at dinner. Where were you?"

We looked at one another and smiled, as full of amiability as a pair of idiots. One really has to be a horse's ass to ask a question like that.

"I went to Cuévano," I said.

"Oh, did you? And what's doing in Cuévano?"

I didn't bother to answer. I went straight to the dining room.

5

When I left my room at five o'clock, Gerardo and Fernando were in the corridor in exactly the same positions as on the afternoon before when I saw them in the patio: Gerardo with arms crossed on his chest and eyebrows drawn together in a frown, Fernando thoughtfully caressing his mustache. This time they were getting the bad news from "The Gringo," who was talking in a low voice, his arms at his sides. Amalia interspersed an occasional comment, moving her hands as though giving zest to the story. Like the day before, Fernando was the first to notice me, but this time it was "The Gringo" whom he poked with his elbow. The four of them turned toward me and smiled. I smiled back, thinking, "Now the four of them know that I went to the mine and brought back ore samples." We said hello; Gerardo's sons came into the patio playing this time with a small rubber ball instead of a soccer ball, a change that made no difference because when my uncle Ramón emerged from his bedroom, pushed by Lucero and Zenaida, the first thing he said was, "Gerardo, make those kids disappear."

Again, as they had done the day before, Gerardo's boys kissed my uncle's hand, and again Lucero had to sponge off the back of it with alcohol.

"Fernando wants to know if the Land Rover gave you any trouble," Gerardo said to me, and added, addressing his brother, "Right, Fernando?"

"Yes, as a matter of fact, I would like to know if the car gave you any trouble," Fernando said, "but, more than anything, if I can have it back now."

My uncle did not give me a chance to answer.

"Marcos is going to need the car tomorrow and the day after," he said.

"It's your car, uncle. Do whatever you want," said Fernando. "It makes no difference to me anyway, whether I have it or not. All I have to do is take out one of the horses and ride, which is very good exercise."

My uncle ignored Fernando and, addressing me, said, "Did you bring what I asked for?"

He winked at me and I understood that he was referring to the samples. I said that I had.

"All right, then, take it to the office right away. I'm in a hurry to see it."

Obviously this was just another device to upset the Tarragona nephews.

"Goodbye, boys," he said to them as Lucero pushed him toward his office.

As I walked through carrying the cement-bag of rocks, Amalia was leaning on the railing looking at a small cloud, "The Gringo" was lighting his cigar again, and Gerardo and Fernando had seated themselves at opposite ends of the wicker settee, each with his legs crossed.

My uncle, sitting at the desk, signalled for me to lock the door with the key, and when I had done so, he indicated that I should put the rocks on the desk-blotter cover.

"They'll scratch the leather," I said.

"It doesn't matter."

I put them on the cover, and my uncle turned on his desk light, opened one of the little drawers, and began poking about in it. Among the objects he removed were the little violet-blue bottle with the medicine dropper and the label that said "Farmacia La Fe," an old watch, and some photographs the subjects of which were too dark to make out. However, I did notice one among them that had crumpled corners and was inscribed "To Estela" in a childish hand. My uncle found what he was looking for and shut the drawer. It was a jeweler's lens that he pushed into the socket of his right eye, the side on which he could control the muscles to hold it in place. He selected one of the rocks and began to examine it.

I was beside the desk. I felt like smoking, took out a cigarette, and was about to light up when, without shifting his attention from the rock he was studying, he ordered, "Don't smoke, it distracts me."

I returned the cigarette—a Delicado—to the pack. Watching my uncle bent over the chunk of cryolite studying it through the jeweler's lens—something I never dreamed he might own—tyrannically forbidding me to smoke, I realized I was fond of him despite the fact that he was what the Chamuca would call a member of the oppressor class.

"Which contains the beryllium?" he asked. "The white or the red?"

"Both. The red is beryllium sulfide, and the white, carbonate."

I gave him a brief summary of how those rocks were formed in the Tertiary, which he interrupted, saying, "How interesting!" He let go of the rock, removed the lens from his eye socket and threw it into the little drawer, which he closed. Once more I was able to see the inscription "To Estela" on the photograph.

He threw himself back in the wheelchair and asked, "What's the next move?"

"You'll have to have the rocks assayed to make sure they are cryolite and of .08 metal content."

"That's my job. What's yours?"

"For the moment, to wait."

"For what?"

"For you to get the results and give me the balance of my nine thousand pesos. The costs and profitability study involves a topographical survey, plans, and calculations. That means I will need money to rent surveying instruments, space for a drafting office, and a car for transportation to and from the mine."

Looking at me with great condescension, my uncle said, "You are mistaken. You won't have to rent surveying instruments, space for a drafting office, or a car. I am going to give you a letter to the Director of the State Department of Public Works in Cuévano, who will lend you the instruments you need without it costing you one centavo; the car you can use for going back and forth to the mine, as you have probably already figured out, is the Land Rover; and, as for a drafting office, ask Lucero to show you the trunk room. If she can draw in there, I don't see why you can't. Finally, so that you won't find any other pretext to hold up the work, I will take it for granted that these rocks are cryolite and that they are of .08 metal content, as you promised, I will pay you the nine thousand pesos right now, and full speed ahead."

That was what I was hoping he would say, but, nonetheless, I asked, "Why are you doing this?"

"Partly because I damn well please and partly because I am an old man with no time to waste."

He opened another one of the little desk drawers and counted out aloud nine thousand-peso notes, one by one, which he put in a pile on the desk next to where my hand was resting. At least an equal number of bills remained in the drawer.

"Why," I asked him, "do you keep money in a drawer without a lock when you have a safe?"

"Because I have financial dealings with all your cousins and if I were to open the safe in front of them they would see the mezcal bottle and I would be condemned to drink distilled water for the rest of my life. Get me?"

After that, he had me make out a receipt that read: "Pursuant to our signed contract . . ." and so forth.

"Come on," Lucero said to me, and started off.

I followed behind as she walked, almost without swinging her arms, her head held high. Her hair was gathered in a bun that left the nape of her neck exposed, and the low neckline of her dress permitted a view of the very fine, tiny golden hairs on her back. The pleasing odor of the perfume she was wearing reached me.

We passed the corridor and front door and entered the service part of the house, beyond the enormous kitchen with its cooking range made of tiles and ceiling blackened by greasy soot. Zenaida had fallen asleep seated on a stool, her head resting against the wall between two pans. On the pantry floor were two sacks of beans and a case of melons, and in Zenaida's room there was a lighted votive candle. We brushed past two locked doors and came to the end of the patio, which had another metal door. When Lucero stopped to open it, I moved forward, slipped my arms under hers, and, placing my hands over her belly, pressed her against me. It was an extremely pleasurable sensation. She did nothing to disengage herself, and laughed. I kissed the nape of her neck and she laughed even more. Then something happened that I was not expecting. Her hands having been left free, she opened the door and let out the dog, which I did not see until he bit me. It was the black dog that had been with her when she went to the henhouse. Between the surprise, the fright, and the pain, I let go of her, upon which she moved away from me, still laughing. I gave the dog a kick and he let go of me, without yelping. He was about to launch another attack, but Lucero said, "Down, Poison!"

The dog and I looked at each other in fury, he all set to bite me again and I to fetch him another kick.

"This way," Lucero said.

The three of us walked on peacefully, as if neither the squeeze, the bite, nor the kick had ever happened. We crossed the little cobbled patio and entered the trunk room. Lucero switched on the light. It was a long whitewashed room with two windows through which my uncle's henhouse and the geraniums on the roof of don Pepe Lara's house were visible in the twilight. The trunks were in one corner, out of the way, and there was an easel, a stool, and a small table next to one of the windows. I was interested in seeing the painting on the easel, which turned out to be a dismal portrait of "The Gringo." I went over to the little table and admired a still life that did not have the slightest merit.

"This is very good," I commented.

Lucero picked up the still life and turned it face down. I looked around the room, studying the possibilities of converting it into a drafting office—any room can be made into a drafting office by moving a table and a lamp into it—and again I said, "This is very good."

I realized that as I was studying the room, Lucero had been studying me.

"I like you," she said.

I was about to take a step toward her but Poison bared his teeth and I held back. Lucero waited for Poison and me to leave the room before turning out the light. As she closed the padlock, I asked, "At what time do you paint?" Not because I was interested in the answer but because I wanted to lend the whole scene an air of authenticity.

"Not any special time. Would it bother you if I painted while you were working?"

"On the contrary, I like to have company."

While Lucero was locking the other door—Poison

was shut inside—I was on the verge of squeezing her
again when the sound of Amalia's voice stopped me.

"How was it?" she wanted to know. "Did you like
the trunk room? Will you be able to work there?"

Her dark-blue, slim, hour-glass figure approached us
in a very solicitous attitude.

That night after supper, following the routine estab-
lished the previous evening, my uncle and I repaired
to his office. Two things worthy of note occurred. One
was that Lucero, not Amalia, brought in the tray with
cognac and mineral water. Instead of leaving it on the
little table that was within our reach, as her mother
had done the night before, Lucero brought it over to
the desk, herself poured out the cognac and mineral
water, and placed the two glasses before us. This required her going back and forth across the room and
bending over twice. After she was gone, my uncle said,
"I have the impression that this young lady is waving
her butt in your face."

He drank three shots of cognac, as he had done the
night before, and smoked like a chimney. The other
interesting thing he said was, "I pretend to be keen
about the mine but all I actually have to look forward
to is death."

He looked really old and sick at that moment.

Why did she say "I like you"? I asked myself later on
when I was in bed. Why, if it is true that she likes me,
did she open the door to the patio so the dog could bite
me? And why did she say "I like you" afterwards? Another question: Why did she kiss me this morning? Did
she really feel like kissing me or was it the only thing
that occurred to her to do when I nearly caught her
red-handed going through my shirt pockets? Furthermore—as I was cogitating there in bed—granted that

Lucero may have found herself in such a tight spot this morning that she had no way out but to kiss me; on the other hand, nothing happened this afternoon to force her to say she liked me if she doesn't like me. My deduction was that she does like me and that this morning, even if she had an ulterior motive, she did want to kiss me. However, countering this theory, of course, is the fact that while I was squeezing her in the patio, she opened the door and let the dog out. She is a very contradictory woman.

I was in the room lying on my back in the dark in one of the twins' beds, covered with a sheet that, in the half-light, I could see raised into a pyramid by my erection. What would the Chamuca say if she saw me in this state over a woman with no ideology? To blot out this disapproving image of the Chamuca, I summoned up the memory of the kiss Lucero had given me and the squeeze I gave her.

The church clock struck a quarter after one, I heard the feathered mules, the bathroom door opening and closing, the toilet being flushed, the bathroom door again, and the mules fading away. Why these sounds should have caused me to conceive a very audacious plan, I don't know. I wondered how long it could take for Amalia to fall fast asleep again. Too late, now, to be drumming up conversations that might clarify the point, such as saying to her, for example: "I suffer from insomnia. What kind of a sleeper are you?" Again, I remembered Lucero kissing me and Lucero setting the glasses down on the little table, and my uncle's remark. I got out of bed at a quarter to two.

I don't know where I got the nerve to walk out into the corridor naked in a house as respectable as my uncle Ramón Tarragona's. Not only naked, but with an erection. Luckily, not even the cenzontle saw me, because Zenaida covers his cage with an old towel. The moon was out. I came to Lucero's bedroom door and turned the knob. I never heard a doorknob—and then the door—move more silently. The sound of the blood pounding in my temples, however, was deafening. I closed the door carefully. It took a little while for me to distinguish the outlines of Lucero's body. She was asleep, sprawled on her belly, arms spread, hands on either side of the pillow, facing the other end of the room, taking up almost the whole bed, which was wide. When I bumped into a chair her breathing changed, when I lifted the covers she moved one leg, and when I got into the bed, she woke up.

"Don't get scared," I said very quietly. "It's me, Marcos."

This was the most dangerous moment. If she yelled, I would be in the soup, but she didn't. She didn't even move. I put my hand on her shoulder, she did not push it away, and I began to feel her body. I discovered then that Lucero slept in a cotton T-shirt and panties. Without changing position, without turning around to look at me, she permitted me to slip my hands under her T-shirt, to fondle her breasts, and to press her against my body so that she would feel my erection. I was positive that in a moment or two I would be having Lucero; at the same time, I realized that I had left the condoms in the dresser drawer in the twins' room, but I was so excited and her body seemed so receptive that I decided to proceed. I put my hands inside her panties and touched her pubic hair, pushed my fingers under the elastic band and tried to slip the panties off. Then Lucero shifted position and brought her legs together.

I never did manage to separate them. First I covered the length of her body with kisses until I reached her toes, then I made believe I had lost interest and turned my back on her, and finally I knelt on the bed, placed my hands on her knees, and tried to pry them apart.

We both put forth our best efforts, but she won out. When the struggle was over, the covers were in a pile on the floor, I was panting, and Lucero was in the fetal position, eyes closed, T-shirt and panties in place. I got off the bed, bumped into the chair again, and, as I opened the door, she spoke for the first time. "Good night," she said.

I was on the verge of slamming the door but instead shut it carefully. I went to the bathroom and peed. I realized that to go back to bed in my condition would be unbearable. Consequently another plan came to mind that was even more dangerous than the previous one. Actually, it was hardly a plan, because I was already carrying it out even before it was conceived. Rather, it was an irresistible impulse. I was inside Amalia's room before I realized it. What a different reception that was! As soon as Amalia heard somebody stumbling into the furniture, she turned on the light. She was wearing a very low-cut nightgown that exposed the upper part of her huge breasts, and she had a cloth tied around her head to keep her hairdo from getting mussed; her mules—they actually did have feathers—were beside the bed. She talked a lot but in a whisper. If I remember correctly, she said, "What's going on? . . . What is the matter with you, Marcos? . . . What do you want? . . . Holy Mother of God! . . . Look at the state you're in! . . . You must be crazy! . . . Think of my reputation! . . . Oh, how wonderful! . . ."

She was quiet, fortunately, after that.

I got back to my room while it was still dark, before Zenaida had gotten up and uncovered the cenzontle. I crawled into bed and slept soundly. I was awakened by the bells ringing for eight o'clock Mass. As soon as I opened my eyes I felt very depressed. What an incredibly stupid thing to have done, I thought. My infidelity to the Chamuca was secondary, because she wouldn't know about it and even if anyone were to tell her she would refuse to believe it. A much more serious possibility to be considered was that my uncle or Lucero might have heard what had gone on in the neighboring room. In a cold sweat, I imagined the scene that might unfold a little later in the dining room: I entering; my uncle, grim-faced because his home had been defiled; Amalia, the medicine dropper in her hand, preparing the medicine, her face flushed with shame; Lucero sniffling. I would have no alternative but to leave the house. The escapade was costing me forty thousand pesos.

However, the other possibility that had to be taken into account was that neither my uncle nor Lucero had been aware of anything. My uncle's house is old and has extremely thick walls of adobe, two coats of plaster, masonry, layers of mortar, and, lastly, wallpaper. A thickness of nearly one meter. I could not recall hearing any sounds when I was in the twins' room other than that of Amalia's heels as she walked in the corridor.

I reviewed the events of the previous night in my mind, trying to analyze them from the auditory standpoint. The bed creaking, the two of us screwing furiously, I snorting, she crying out and, at the end, emitting a strange, long-drawn-out moan that sounded like a cow mooing. I was unable to clarify anything but did reach the conclusion that I had spent a very satisfactory night. The worst that could happen, I figured, was that I would have to leave. So be it! I would take the nearly ten thousand pesos my uncle had given me, pick up the Chamuca in Jerez, and go on to Half Moon Beach and Hotel Aurora where we would stay until the money was used up. Then, we would see.

As I stepped out of my room I met Lucero leaving hers. The way she looked at me dispelled any fears I had. Obviously she wasn't holding against me what had happened in her room, nor did she have any idea of what had taken place in Amalia's.

"What kind of a night did you have?" she asked with a smile.

Without waiting for an answer, she walked off in a way that recalled to my mind what my uncle had said the night before: ". . . this young lady is waving her butt in your face."

When I entered the dining room, my uncle had finished his breakfast and was picking his teeth. He left off doing that as soon as he saw me, and pointed to a sealed envelope that lay on the table next to my place. I felt a shock. Had he realized what went on last night and written me a letter telling me never to darken his door again? I was on the point of opening the letter when my uncle said, "Don't be a jackass! It's not for you. It's for the Director of Public Works in Cuévano, telling him that you are my nephew and that I would appreciate his lending you any surveying instruments you might need."

"Thanks, uncle," I said with relief, leaving the letter on the table. "I'll go and get them today."

Amalia entered at that moment. How different women seem to one if one has made love with them. She didn't look so ridiculous to me anymore. She had painted her eyelids blue and put mascara on her lashes, and she wore a thin white dress. She asked me the same question as her daughter: "What kind of a night did you have?"

When I said "very good," she laughed throatily and said, "What would you like for your breakfast?"

She herself—as she told me afterwards—prepared the eggs Mexican-style, fried the beans, and heated the tortillas, and she brought the breakfast to the table.

"I've never seen her so full of energy," remarked my

uncle when Amalia went to the kitchen for the sweet rolls.

She came back, sat down at the table to watch me eat, and spoke of certain birds she had seen in the fields, saying, "They are teenie-weenie things with almost all-black little heads and wings, and their little breasties are all brown."

"They are called swallows," said my uncle, who had been listening incredulously to her description.

What Amalia was trying to describe were, in fact, swallows, which nest in the beams of the arcade and fly sometimes by moving their wings and sometimes by gliding with the power of the impulse. Amalia was astonished that it could be possible that she should have lived so many years without knowing what a swallow was, although she had seen them so often. I found the way in which she reacted and the heartiness of her laugh—I was able to see the roof of her mouth—quite engaging. I noted that my uncle was watching her in silence. I loaded refried beans and egg into a tortilla, and as I bit into it I thought: "Amalia may be very dumb but she has a good heart," and, a moment later, "Nobody is going to get me out of this house until my uncle gives me the forty thousand pesos I have coming to me."

My uncle asked that as long as I was going to Cuévano I take don Pepe Lara with me, who had to go there to look after various matters, among them delivering the cryolite samples to the assay laboratory.

When I drove up to don Pepe's house in the Land Rover, he was already waiting at the door. He was dressed up for the trip to the capital of the state in a dark-gray suit and a newer hat than the one he usually wore. He had put the cryolite samples into a sisal sack that was cleaner and more presentable than the cement-bag I had been using. Doña Jacinta came out to say goodbye to him as though he were setting off on a long journey, and not to a city only forty kilometers away.

"God be with you!" said doña Jacinta as the car drove away.

I waited until we came to a straight stretch in the highway before asking don Pepe the question I had prepared for him: "Who is or was Estela?"

He turned his head and peered at me. He had never looked more like an owl. Obviously he did not like the question and was not sure how to answer me.

"Where did you see that name?"

I told him that when my uncle opened one of his desk drawers the day before, I had caught a glimpse of a photograph that was inscribed "To Estela."

As though facing up to the inevitable, don Pepe said, "Estela was your aunt Leonor."

"What do you mean, my aunt Leonor?"

"That's the name they called her at the place where she used to work."

"Where did my aunt work?"

"I thought you knew."

I didn't, but it always seemed odd to me that my aunt Leonor, a poor girl from a farm, should have married my uncle Ramón, a wealthy hacienda owner from the time he was a young man. My mother had always been vague whenever this point came up. "Your aunt Leonor," she would say, "went to work in Cuévano where she met don Ramón." Nobody had ever told me at what my aunt Leonor worked, but I had had an idea that she was a saleslady in a dry-goods store.

"Did my aunt work in a whorehouse?"

Don Pepe hunched up his shoulders as high as he possibly could, as though to cover his ears with them and shut out the words.

"Don't call it that! It was more like a boarding house."

"Where young ladies stayed . . ."

"Right!"

"And gentlemen came to visit them."

"Listen, Marcos, I admired and respected your aunt Leonor more than any other woman I ever knew in my whole life."

"I have wonderful memories of her too. That's why I want you to tell me where she worked."

Don Pepe huddled into his chair as though he felt cold and said, his eyes focussed fixedly ahead, "Your aunt came to work in a house located in the Malaquitas alley that belonged to a señora Aurelia. Ramón met her there and fell in love with her. They got married and lived happily until, unfortunately, she died, which was the worst calamity that could have happened to Ramón. The photograph you saw in Ramón's desk inscribed 'To Estela' must have been one the other girls gave her the day she left and went to live in Muérdago in the house Ramón bought for her in the San José section."

Don Pepe's revelation, rather than shocking me, made the figure of my aunt more interesting and clarified a great deal about her. But, of course, it did not stop my saying to myself from then on, whenever something goes sour and I get the blues: I come from up in the hills, my dad was a loser, everybody calls me El Negro, my only relative who got rich started out by being a whore. Life has handed me a screwing.

6

We parked the Land Rover outside the Mine Registry building again and went up on foot by way of Campomanes. When we reached the corner, don Pepe stopped and, stretching out his hand, said, "Thanks a lot for the lift, Marcos boy."

I offered to pick him up anywhere he liked in a couple of hours and bring him back to Muérdago with me, but he said he preferred to return by bus because he had a number of errands to take care of and didn't know when he would be through. That suited me fine, because even though I liked the old fellow, with him along, I wouldn't be able to stop off at the mine on the way, if I should want to. We said goodbye and he went along The Turk's Street in the direction of the university, where the mineral assay laboratory is located. I crossed Liberty Plaza and went into the State Office Building.

I was amazed at the power of my uncle's influence in Cuévano. All I had to do was present his letter to the girl at the reception desk and inside of two minutes I was being received by the Director of Public Works himself, who, instead of remaining seated behind his desk, came to the door of his office to usher me in. He was a prognathic old engineer by the name of Requena who had been one of my professors at the School of Mines. When I mentioned this circumstance to him, he pretended that he remembered me, saying, "You were an outstanding student."

A falsehood. I was never anything of the kind.

We sat down. He wanted to know how my uncle was. "Somewhat better," I told him, "considering the seriousness of his condition." I assumed an air of importance befitting a trusted nephew of my uncle. After he had read through the letter with respectful attention he said, "Anything don Ramón asks me for is his. Naturally, the same holds true for you. What instruments will you be needing?"

I handed him my list. It specified the basic equipment for making a topographical survey that would be precise but not require anything out of the ordinary. Engineer Requena asked me a few questions. Obviously he was curious about what my uncle wanted a survey for. I let him think it concerned laying out metes and bounds of some properties of his. I mentioned nothing about a mine or cryolite deposit, since he would know perfectly well that such an evaluation called for borings and those are almost impossible to fake. My answers—all complete fabrications—seemed to satisfy him, and he concluded the interview by filling out a requisition and signing it.

I was still congratulating myself on how easily I had bamboozled the engineer when I arrived at the supply room to pick up the instruments and discovered that the person in charge was a fellow by the name of Malvidio who had worked with me at the Planning Office. Never having seen me without a beard, he did not recognize me at first, but as soon as he noticed the name on the requisition he made the connection.

"Negro!" he said. "It's great to see you!"

I acted as though I were delighted to see him and we gave each other an embrace. This sonofabitch—I said to myself—is the only one who is going to know, when my description comes out in the newspapers, which should be soon, that Marcos González, alias "El Negro," who worked in the Planning Office and is a fugitive from justice, is the same person who is going around the state of Plan de Abajo making surveys with instruments borrowed from the Office of Public Works. Malvidio, who is redheaded and always rubbed me the wrong way, invited me to his house for dinner. I declined with a firmness bordering on rudeness. If he is going to turn me in, I figured, he is going to do it whether I go to his house or not, and so I preferred to let him feel offended and spare myself his company.

Malvidio was offended but nevertheless he did have a couple of men carry the transit, poles, level rods, and tripod to the Land Rover. I handed them twenty pesos and they went off very pleased. I put the transit in the trunk and locked it. I then bought the Mexico City newspapers and went to read them at the Flor de Cué-vano, where, incidentally, the coffee is just as bad as it used to be when I was a student. I was relieved to see that neither the Chamuca nor I was in the papers, nor was the Globo fire mentioned. I left the table to put in a long distance call to Jerez, Angel Valdés again asking to speak to señorita Medina.

"How are you?" I asked the Chamuca.

"Still missing you."

"Be patient. Everything is going well. It's a matter of one week. My uncle will be giving me the money at that time, I'll come by for you, and we'll be off to Half Moon Beach together."

Then, suddenly, it dawned on me that I had left the Chamuca with sixty-one pesos four days ago and that she must be having problems.

"I'll be sending you money today," I told her. "A thousand pesos."

She thanked me. Apparently she was pleased. On hearing her voice, which sounded so frank, so unaffected, and comparing it with Amalia's or Lucero's, I felt an upsurge of love for her that was stronger than ever and I said, "I love you. Tell me you love me."

"I love you," she said.

We said goodbye. I had hung up and was about to leave the booth when the figure of a man passing by in the street caught my attention.

"Could that be Pancho?" I wondered.

A chill ran up and down my spine. While the cashier checked the cost of my call, I went to the door and saw the same man again crossing the street. He did resemble Pancho but was thinner, if I remembered correctly. I paid my check and the charge for the call, returned to the table, gathered up the newspapers, and walked over to Constitution Square again to throw them into a trash can there. I got into the Land Rover, started it up, and drove toward Cuévano. Riding along the highway, I realized that the scare the supposed Pancho had thrown into me had made me forget the thousand pesos I was going to send the Chamuca. I had intended to go to the bank and buy a draft in her name against the branch in Jerez. Now I realized I would have to let it go until the following day, since it would be impossible to get to Muérdago before one-thirty, when the banks close.

On reaching the mine I had the feeling that the place was deserted, but when I climbed out of the Land Rover and started toward the entrance, I heard El Colorado's voice behind me.

"Hey!" he shouted.

He startled me. I turned around and saw that El Colorado had made a stronghold of the Spaniard's house. He had constructed a barricade with stones in one of the windows, out of which the barrel of the carbine was poking. He was standing in the doorway, having just stood up from a small chair and spat out a mouthful of pulp from the sugar-cane stalk he was holding. I walked over to him and we shook hands.

"Help me fetch some things from the car," I said to him.

We took out the unwieldy instruments and put them in the Spaniard's house in one of the rooms that still had some roof over it. All I left in the Land Rover was the transit in its case, which I planned to carry in and out of my uncle's house in order to impress everybody with the importance of the work I was doing. After we had finished carting the instruments, El Colorado stood looking down at the ground before imparting the news to me.

"Some jerk came around and I winged him with the carbine."

"How bad was he hit?"

"So-so. I aimed at a leg but got him in the arm. A little blood squirted out but not enough to stop him from jumping into his car and taking off like a bat out of hell."

He showed me the stains of almost black dried blood on the grass.

"Was he a very tall guy with a very long neck who was wearing a red and green shirt?"

"That's the one."

"And he was driving a small white car?"

"That's the car."

I thought: Despite what had happened at night and the breakfast she fixed for me, Amalia had told "The Gringo" that I was taking don Pepe to Cuévano, and that gave him the idea that nobody would be at the mine in the morning.

I gave El Colorado two hundred pesos more.

I got back to Muérdago in time for lunch. "The Gringo's" car was parked in front of the door, which spelled trouble. I took out the transit case and banged the knocker.

"They're in the corridor," said Zenaida, as she opened the door.

Everybody was looking at me, reprovingly, I thought. "The Gringo" had changed his red and green shirt for a green and red one, and his arm was in a sling. He sat in the rocking chair, an expression of pain on his face. Amalia stood beside him, her arm resting on his shoulder as though she were trying to absorb some of the hurt.

"What happened to your arm?" I asked "The Gringo."

He just clenched his teeth. Amalia answered me, "Imagine, he was chasing a dog and fell down and sprained it very badly."

I realized that there would be no recriminations and as I breathed a sigh of relief, I noticed that the other three Tarragonas were in the corridor, Alfonso in shirt-sleeves, arms crossed, leaning against the railing, Gerardo and Fernando sitting in the wicker settee, smoking. Despite signs of conviviality, such as half-empty tequila glasses and sucked limes, the atmosphere was tense. I put the transit case on the floor. Everybody looked at it with curiosity but no one asked what it was. As I straightened up, Lucero appeared at the dining-room door with a glass of tequila in one hand and a dish of cheese in the other. Smiling, she handed me the tequila and offered me the cheese. Then I realized that the most striking aspect of the assemblage was the absence of my uncle.

"Where's my uncle?" I asked.

All eyes shifted away from me. There was silence until Amalia, after casting a questioning glance toward her brothers, said, "He's in his office."

"He's talking to *licenciado* Zorrilla," said Alfonso.

"I don't know who *licenciado* Zorrilla is," I said.

"He is the most important notary in town," said Gerardo.

"It seems my uncle is writing his will," said Fernando.

I sat down. Lucero passed the cheese around. "The Gringo" groaned as he shifted in the rocker. Fernando began to jiggle his leg nervously, but since it was making the sofa creak he had to stop. Alfonso walked back and forth in the corridor, not saying a word. Amalia busied herself by collecting the used dishes. No sooner did someone flick the ashes off a cigarette than she tried to remove the ashtray. Lucero came and went with dishes of cheese.

"They've been in there for two hours now," said Gerardo, consulting his watch.

It was as though the family's favorite dog had slipped out into the street.

I got up and went into the dining room for another drink. Lucero entered behind me and squeezed herself between the sideboard and me.

"Let me serve you," she said, taking the bottle out of my hand.

She filled my glass with tequila, took it from me, tasted it, returned it to me, and laughed. We stayed there that way, pressed together, I against her, she against the cabinet, looking into each other's eyes without speaking. Fortunately nobody came in at that moment.

When we got back to the corridor, my uncle was coming out of the office, his wheelchair being pushed by three white-haired men, all dressed in suits with vests and wearing neckties. The four of them were laughing at the joke about the hyena. I, being familiar with my uncle's little secrets, took it for granted that they had been drinking mezcal. The joviality of the old men contrasted sharply with the identical tight smiles on the faces of my four cousins. On noticing my presence, my uncle introduced me to his friends, saying, "This is Marcos, my other nephew, about whom we have already spoken."

I gathered that he must have said something nice about me to them because they greeted me very affably. They were *licenciado* Zorrilla, who carried a leather briefcase, Dr. Canalejas, the ends of whose mustache were twisted upward, and a third man, whom I had already met, Paco of the Casino. Amalia offered them an apéritif, which they declined, and then they took their leave. It was interesting that before stepping out, *licenciado* Zorrilla said to my uncle as he slapped his briefcase, "I'll see to it that this document is registered today without fail."

We all listened with interest. We realized that the will had been made out. When the old men were gone, Alfonso asked my uncle, solicitously, "How did you make out with the notary? Did you have any problems?"

"None whatsoever. Everything worked out fine."

He wanted to know what was in the case I had brought in. I opened it and took out the transit.

"That's something for you to keep in mind, Fernando," my uncle said. "We must take advantage of having an instrument like that and an engineer on hand to set up the metes and bounds of The Yoke. Get together with Marcos, take him out to the hacienda one of these days, and have him tell us how much he'll charge for the job."

"If you think metes and bounds are good for anything, I'll have it done."

Nothing further was said of the will.

After lunch, instead of going to Amalia's room to take his siesta as he did every afternoon, "The Gringo," who was obviously still feeling bad, wanted to go home.

"But you're not well enough to drive," Amalia said.

My other cousins had left and I was the only able-bodied man in the house.

"Let Marcos take him," my uncle said.

And that was how "The Gringo," who did not want to be taken home by me, and I, who did not want to take him home, ended up together in the little white car. "The Gringo" explained the route I should take and then asked me, "Do you know how I happened to come to Muérdago?"

"No."

"Take a guess. I'll give you three chances."

"I haven't the slightest idea."

"I was hunting for Pancho Villa's treasure."

One really had to be a jerk, I thought, to go looking for Pancho Villa's treasure in a place where Pancho Villa had never been.

"Yes, I had reason to think that the treasure was buried in a little church in Comales."

"Was it there?"

"No, but do you know what I did find in Muérdago?"

"I told you I had no idea."

"I found Amalia."

"I understand."

But I didn't understand a thing. I couldn't make head or tail of the conversation. When we arrived at his house and got out of the car, "The Gringo" said, making a motion with his head, "Come on in."

"Thanks, but I have a lot to do."

"I want to show you my firearms collection."

I went in and saw the collection. "The Gringo" had rifles and shotguns of all sizes and calibers. He explained which kind should be used for killing a deer at close quarters and which at a distance and which was the right gun for shooting quail.

"Do you like hunting?" he asked.

"Not at all," I told him.

"I invite you to go shooting agachonas next Sunday on the Bagre River bank."

I was about to tell him that I didn't care for agachonas even in *mole* sauce, and cared much less for having to go to the Bagre River to shoot them, to say nothing of the company. But I didn't have the nerve and came out with something very weak, like: "I don't think I'll be able to make it."

It seems that although "The Gringo" could speak Spanish, he understood only what he wanted to, because as he was showing me out he said, "I'll stop by for you at seven o'clock on Sunday." Then, he added something I didn't understand but which gave me a chill: "I never forget anything."

That afternoon, I rearranged the trunk room and turned it into a drafting office by adding a table I found in the pantry and a floor lamp that had once been in the living room. Zenaida swept, dusted, and helped me shift things around. After she left I went to work.

The job I intended to deliver to my uncle was going to have four phases: first, the laying out of the polygonation on the aerial map, a matter of half an hour; second, the measurement of the data obtained from the polygonation and their transferral to a field book, one day's work; third, the drawing of a configuration of the Covadonga mine and surrounding points on the basis of the field-book data—this configuration was going to be similar to the aerial map but would contain details that did not appear on it or, of course, actually exist anywhere—three days' work; fourth and last, based on the data from the field book, the filling up of several sheets of graph paper with equivocal calculations, such as computation of volumes and incidence ratios, which would give the impression that the mine was rich but required a larger investment than initially estimated, another day's work. The final recommendation I planned to make to my uncle was that he should *not* invest. I hoped that, being grateful for my having saved him from making a bad investment, he would hand over the forty thousand pesos that were coming to me under the terms of the contract, I would pick up the Chamuca, and we would go to Half Moon Beach to stay at the Aurora Hotel together for six months.

I had finished the polygonation and begun to make up the field book when I heard footsteps in the cobblestone patio and a knock on the door, which was ajar.

"Come in," I said, hoping it was Lucero.

It was Alfonso. Behind him in the patio were Gerardo and Fernando. Even though he saw that I was working at a table covered with papers, he asked, "Are you very busy?"

"Sort of."

"Never mind. Leave what you are doing for some other time. We have to talk to you about something very important. Come to the California with us."

The California Bar was a long narrow room with greenish lighting that made the customers look like cadavers. The decorations included a mural of a desert with cactuses, seating was in leather chairs, and the heaviest cuspidors I have ever seen stood around the floor. There was a trio of singing guitarists who played without stopping.

My cousins ordered rum and *Squirt*. Gerardo warned me, "Don't ask for imported stuff in this place. You'll be getting a pig in a poke."

I ordered a Cuba libre. When we were served, everybody took a swallow of his drink and, finally, Alfonso spoke. "I was hoping," he said, to fill me in, "that my uncle's will would be filed for probate, because I have a connection in the office of his notary who would have informed me what was in it by now. Unfortunately that is not the case. It seems that what happened this morning was that my uncle wrote out a will by hand, put it in an envelope, and sealed it with sealing wax. The other three in the office with him attested that my uncle had drawn up the document of his own free will and that he was of sound mind when he wrote it, but that they don't know its provisions, either. All they say at the Registry is that my uncle's will is in a sealed envelope in *licenciado* Zorrilla's safe."

Gerardo took the floor. "That is to say, we are in the same boat as before. We know my uncle has made a decision but no one knows what it is and there isn't anybody we can ask."

"We could ask my uncle," said Fernando.

The three of them looked at me expectantly. I groped for a comment that wouldn't obligate me and, not finding one, I said, "I understand."

"The time we spoke about this matter," Gerardo said to me, "I asked you to tell us, as soon as you knew, what my uncle had left you so that we could make accounts. What news do you have?"

"None," I answered. "My uncle hasn't said a word to me."

Alfonso took over. "Let's not worry about what my uncle might tell you. How much do you calculate your share of the inheritance is worth? Tell us right now, because my brothers and I are ready to buy you out this minute. Throw out a figure."

This was the moment when I should have said one, two, or three hundred thousand pesos, which would have meant one, two, or three years with the Chamuca in the Aurora Hotel at Half Moon Beach. But then serious doubts entered my mind: Maybe, at some point, I should ask for a million; and, something even more worrisome: perhaps the best thing would be to not sell, and wait for my uncle to die. In other words, I was reasoning like a petit bourgeois, and that paralyzed me.

"I don't know," I said. "I have to think about it."

"Think it over tonight and let us know tomorrow," Alfonso said. "The deal we have to arrange is very simple. We hand you the money and you sign a paper renouncing your inheritance."

"Provided," Gerardo interrupted, "the price you ask seems reasonable to us."

"And taking into account the possibility," Fernando added, "that my uncle won't leave you anything."

Not until Fernando made that remark did I realize that there was no chance that my uncle would be leaving me nothing. If there had been—I reasoned—these three wouldn't be sitting here trying to buy my share.

When I returned to the house, my uncle was in his office playing chess with Lucero, who was evidently winning. When he saw me come in, an expression of relief crossed his face and he said, "It's a good thing you're back. I wanted to talk to you. We'll finish the game some other time, Lucero. Meanwhile, bring Marcos a bottle of cognac."

Lucero put the chessboard in a corner and left the office.

"You went drinking with your cousins, didn't you?" said my uncle when we were alone.

"How did you know?"

"Lucero saw you leave with them and you look a little bleary-eyed."

Lucero returned with the tray and put it on the desk. She poured my uncle's mineral water into a tumbler and the cognac into a snifter, and leaned over twice to serve us and to show off her ass. As soon as she was out of the room, he tossed off my drink in a gulp.

"I had a terrible thirst," he said, holding out the snifter for a refill.

"Why don't you keep a bottle of the stuff in your safe?" I asked.

"It wouldn't do any good. I like company to drink with."

He then opened the safe and took out one of the used glasses, from which I drank. When I asked him what was so urgent that he wanted to talk to me about, he said it was nothing, that he just wanted a drink.

"I have a touchy question to ask you," I said to him.

"Let's see if it's anything I feel like answering."

"It's this: My cousins are offering to buy out my share of the inheritance from me."

"Let's go slow. What share of what inheritance?"

"They think you left me something in the will you made this morning."

"They do?"

I looked at him closely but could tell nothing from his face that might indicate whether my cousins' supposition was right or wrong.

I went on. "They are offering me a sum of money now to give up my inheritance and get out of the picture."

"Not a bad idea. In your cousins' place, I think I would do the same."

"The question I want to ask you is a double one. First, would it be to my interest to sell my inheritance and, second, in case it is, how much should I ask for?"

My uncle answered without hesitation. "I advise you to sell. Ask a price that sounds very high to you and make them pay as much as possible. But let me warn you, whatever you get from your cousins, you will be coming out ahead of the game."

I had been afraid this conversation was going to be painful for my uncle, but it turned out to be much more so for me, because what he had just finished telling me was that the value of my inheritance was solely in the imaginations of my cousins—since he had not left me anything.

I was dreaming of columns of figures, of the names of the points of the polygonation and the sightings, of distances, azimuths, magnetic bearings, and so on. When I opened my eyes I realized I was in the twins' room. I felt very warm, particularly my back. I felt as though I had put on a very heavy overcoat. Another strange sensation was of something hard between my ribs and the mattress that was not my arm. Hands that were not my hands were caressing my prick, and somebody began sticking a tongue into my ear. Somebody was on top of me. I was about to say, "Lucero, my love!" when I realized that the weight on me was very heavy.

"Amalia, my love!" I said.

The moist kiss I received told me I had guessed right.

7

The next day, April 18, at 10:30 A.M., I wrote the following note, which is included because I consider it a faithful reflection of my state of mind at that moment.

"My uncle Ramón must be picturing me clambering over the hills, dragging the transit through the brush, focussing the lens, trying to read the vernier with the magnifying glass, noting down columns of figures in the field book, and so on. He is mistaken. I am sitting in a pond up to my hips in warm water, writing this note. The transit is in its case and my clothes are under a mesquite tree. I am naked, seated on a kind of mud throne in front of a rock sticking out of the water that I am using as a desk. I could have finished writing up the field book here in no time if I had brought the aerial map with me from the trunk room. Too bad! The pond is at the center of The Cauldron, and rising around me are the four identical hills, named The Jib, The Bib, The Northern Tit, and The Hill Without a Name. I never forget their names, but I had to get El Colorado to tell me a little while ago which hill corresponded to which name. This is very important for the work I am doing since it lends authenticity. Now, besides the fact that the mine is dug into the slope of The Hill Without a Name, I also know that the hot spring pours out of the foot of The Northern Tit, and that the hotel and the settlement are on the depression between The Jib and The Bib.

"The pond still stinks of sulfur just like when I was

a kid, and there are still aquatic plants growing on the bottom that we used to tie around our heads to make ourselves look like sea monsters. The reeds and huisaches must be taller now, because formerly the owner of the hotel could watch us from the second-story window as we played but now she wouldn't be able to see a thing because of the wall of vegetation between the hotel and the pond.

"I came here today not out of a sense of duty but to kill time, since it would be assumed that I should be leaving the house in the morning to do field work. I fully deserve this breather I am taking, particularly in view of the night Amalia put me through. Could anyone have dreamed that I would be cheating on the Chamuca, to whom I had never been unfaithful before, with a woman, shall I say, of ripe years—Amalia must be pushing forty-five—whom I had always considered ridiculous? Now as I am getting to know her she doesn't seem so ridiculous to me anymore. To tell the truth, I was very appreciative of the way she awakened me last night."

From there, I went to Cuévano and picked up the "nonregistration certificate" at the Mine Registry for the Covadonga, Municipality of Las Tuzas, State of Plan de Abajo. This express service was achieved with two hundred pesos I had slipped the head of archives, who at first wanted me to wait two months until he felt like searching the records. According to the document, the Spaniard who had operated the mine for the extraction of manganese ore was named José Isabel Tenazas Archundia, and he wasn't Spanish, having been born in El Oro, State of Mexico. I hope—I thought—my uncle doesn't take it into his head to show the paper to any miner, who would know that beryllium is never found where there is manganese.

I bought the Mexico City newspapers again, and again

went to read them at a table in the Flor de Cuévano, and again nothing appeared on the Globo fire. I had gotten up and gone to the cashier's desk to place another long-distance call to the Chamuca, when in a corner of the cafe—from which it was fortunately not likely that I had been seen—I saw the man who looked like Pancho or, on further consideration, most likely was Pancho. I had to make a determined effort to keep myself from dashing out of the place. I stopped only long enough to drop a bill on the table, crossed Constitution Square, got into the car, and didn't begin to calm down until I was on the highway. I realized, then, that if the police had checked my file at the Planning Office, they would have had no trouble in connecting me with the city of Cuévano, since my records would show that I had attended the School of Mines there. I decided that the wisest course would be not to set foot in Cuévano again. Muérdago, on the other hand, seemed safe, unless it might have occurred to Pancho—if it was Pancho—to interview my former teachers, which would lead him to old Requena, who would show him the letter from my uncle. This possibility, frankly, seemed remote. It appeared to be a very ticklish situation and now urgent to get my hands on the money to take me to the Chamuca and the Aurora Hotel at Half Moon Beach. At this point in my deliberations I remembered that the new scare Pancho had thrown into me had made me forget to send the money I promised the Chamuca. And it was Friday and ten minutes after one.

Amalia had Zenaida move my place at the dinner table. Instead of seating me next to "The Gringo," she put me on the other side next to Lucero. "So that I can look at you better," Amalia told me when we were alone, in explanation of the change. "If you are on the same side as I am, I can't see you because my husband's pumpkin head is in the way."

This time the change had a result Amalia was unaware of. Hidden by the tablecloth, Lucero slipped off her sandal and rubbed little caresses on my ankle with her toes. She served me more than the usual number of tacos, and my uncle protested, saying, "How come you gave Marcos two tacos and me only one?"

"How's your arm?" I asked "The Gringo," who was still wearing the sling.

"Better," he said. "I expect it will be in shape on Sunday for shooting agachonas."

"I'd forgotten we were going hunting," I confessed.

"Better remember, because I never forget anything," warned "The Gringo."

When I heard him say that a second time, again, it gave me a very uneasy feeling.

"I'll ask for a million," I was thinking as I pushed open the door of the California Bar, "but if they offer a hundred thousand, I'll take it."

My cousins were in a corner surrounded by a trio of guitarists singing "Leave Me As I Was" with great feeling. Alfonso motioned to me to come over and when I reached the table, he said, "Just listen to that. Isn't it marvelous?"

"Be cautious," I said to myself. "As long as they don't bring up the matter, don't you say a word. Act as though you don't remember why you came. After all, you have the whole night before you for bargaining."

I realized that my cousins had already been in the place for some time. They weren't exactly drunk, but very emotional.

"Leave Me As I Was" is a song about a man who is having a very unhappy love affair because women aren't the way he expected them to be. When the girl is saying goodbye, he begs her to leave him the way he was before he knew her, "without love, without pain, without anything."

"Oh, mother!" exclaimed Gerardo.

When the singers moved on to another table, Gerardo leaned over toward us and said in a confidential tone, "I am going to tell something to you two because you are my brothers and to you because you are my cousin and come from the capital and are a man of the world."

I was expecting him to talk about the inheritance, but instead he told us about something that had happened to him in La Cañada, a town near Muérdago. The judge there got sick and Gerardo, out of friendship, agreed to take his place temporarily and hear several urgent cases for him. When he arrived in La Cañada he went into the courthouse and sat down at the judge's desk, and the secretary came in with the files.

"You want to know the truth?" he asked the three of us. "When I saw this girl, I felt like an idiot. I said to myself, 'Where do they make such women and where do they keep them that I never knew one like this when I was single?'"

Her name was Angelita and she was twenty-two years old. Three days later, Gerardo proposed to her in these terms: "I don't know what your commitments are, Angelita, but I must have you."

She was unmarried, lived with her mother, and said that she had no ties. My cousin Gerardo had her that night in one of the motels on the highway to Pedrones.

"I'll be honest with you. Angelita is not a very cultured person, but the hours I spent with her that night and afterwards opened a new life for me."

They were happy, according to Gerardo, until one

night when, after having been at the motel, he came home, went into the bedroom, turned on the lamp to undress, and saw his wife asleep in the double bed.

"To see her there looking so peaceful," Gerardo said, "believing the lie I had told her, that I would be home late because I was conducting several confrontations that had turned out to be very difficult to handle, I said to myself, 'You are a villain, because the woman sleeping there peacefully before you, who gave you six children and twenty years of tranquility, who took care of you when you had the d.t.'s, is your true mate!' Boys, do you know what my decision was? To put an end to my relations with Angelita the very next day."

"You did the right thing, brother," said Fernando. "Adulteries lead to nothing but misfortune."

By that time, it appeared from Gerardo's narrative, his work in La Cañada had been completed, and one of the factors that contributed to his decision was the half-hour he had to spend travelling from Muérdago to La Cañada.

"The following day," the story went on, "I had Angelita go into the file room where I followed her and closed the door. I said to her, 'Whatever there was between us is over, Angelita. You are young and I don't want to stand in the way of your future.' To smooth over any possible hard feelings, I offered her a thousand pesos. And what do you think she answered? That I owed her five thousand because she was a virgin when she met me."

"Why, that bitch!" said Alfonso, outraged.

"I gave her the money," he went on.

"You did the wrong thing," said Fernando. "A woman who sets a price on matters of love doesn't deserve one centavo."

"I realize she didn't deserve the money, but I didn't

want her coming around to the house someday and telling my wife what went on at the motel on the road to Pedrones."

"What you should have done," advised Alfonso, "was to appear before the agent of the Public Prosecutor's Office and make a deposition: 'I am a judge and señorita so-and-so is trying to blackmail me.' That would have thrown such a scare into her she wouldn't have bothered you again."

"I still haven't told you the worst," said Gerardo. "Angelita has a fiancé now and they often come to Muérdago together. Sometimes I see them walking through the arcade where my courtroom is."

"I wouldn't put up with such a thing," said Fernando. "I would come out of the courtroom and shoot the two of them dead."

"When I see her arm in arm with another man, I realize I still love her and I feel terrible, as though they were putting a knife into me."

"You're doing the wrong thing, brother," said Alfonso. "Particularly knowing that she is a worthless woman."

"Who would ever have believed," Gerardo concluded, "that at forty-seven years of age I could become a slave of passion."

"I want the singers to come over here," demanded Alfonso.

"I want them to sing 'The One Who Went Away' for me," demanded Gerardo.

The trio came over and sang not just "The One Who Went Away," but a lot of songs. I got up. Gerardo's story had upset me, partly because I had had a number of rums, but mainly because certain aspects of it were too close to home for comfort. I went to the bar and asked the bartender to put through a call for me to a number in Jerez. Since he knew my cousins I didn't want to chance using a false name, and gave my own.

"I didn't send the money I promised," I told the Chamuca when she answered, "but I'll wire it to you tomorrow without fail."

"Where are you?" she asked.

I realized she could hear the voices of the trio who at that moment were singing: "It's not for lack of love/ I adore you with all my soul . . ." and so on.

"I'm closing an important deal with my cousins."

It wasn't exactly an agreeable conversation. I could understand that the Chamuca must be tired of waiting for me and had gotten the impression that I was having a good time in Muérdago.

When I returned to the table, Gerardo had fallen into a profound state of melancholy. Fernando helped him to his feet and took him home. I stayed on at the California with Alfonso in the hope that he would get around to discussing the inheritance. Vain hope. This was the night of the secretaries. Even though it was only eleven-thirty, Alfonso wanted to bring a daybreak serenade to his. "Elenita," he said to me, "the one you met."

I understood that their relations went beyond the office.

He hired the trio, had the waiter load two bottles of Bacardi, ice, glasses, and mixers into the Galaxy, and paid the bill, including my phone call. We drove with singers, guitars, and bottles to a pretentiously shoddy development called Muérdago Heights.

Alfonso and I stayed back, standing next to the Galaxy in a dark street drinking rum and *Squirt*, while the musicians advanced some twenty meters until they were under a colonial-style carved window, on the other side of which, according to Alfonso, Elenita slept. They began to sing, first "Las Mañanitas" and then "Don't go out on the street, child/because the perfidious wind/ toying with your dress/might outline your form . . ." and so on.

At that point, a car went by and one of its passengers called out, "Good night, *licenciado.*"

"Holy shit!" said Alfonso, as the car drove away. "Now I've really got my ass in a sling! The wife of that man who went by is a friend of my wife's, and she's sure as hell going to tell her that her husband saw me serenading in Muérdago Heights!"

He made signs to the musicians to hurry and finish the song they were singing. They obeyed, cutting a chorus. Alfonso hustled the four of us back into the Galaxy and we drove to the other end of the city, where we stopped in front of a modern house of spectacular ugliness.

"This house is your house," he said to me as we got out of the car. He told the musicians, "Okay, boys, sing a little number for my dear wife."

They repeated "Don't go out on the street, child . . ." and so on.

Very pleased with himself, Alfonso explained to me, "If anyone were to ask me what I was doing up in Muérdago Heights, I can say I had to go all the way out there to hire a trio."

I got back to the house fed up with my cousins. Including Amalia. I took off my Argentine boots at the entrance, went to my room trying not to make any noise, and locked the door. I was sound asleep when a slight sound awakened me. Somebody was trying to open the door. Could it be Amalia, or Lucero? I wondered. Suppose I opened the door and it turned out to be Amalia. Bad. But suppose I didn't open it and it was Lucero. Bad, too. Whoever was at the door got me out of my dilemma because the noise stopped. The immediate problem was resolved, but not the mystery. I lay awake thinking: Was it Amalia who wanted in or could it have been Lucero? Then I fell asleep.

In the morning, I was under the shower, my head

covered with lather, when the bathroom door opened.
I lifted a corner of the shower curtain and saw Amalia,
dressed all in white. For a moment, I thought she had
entered thinking the bathroom was free and that as
soon as she saw that I was in the shower she would
leave. That is not what happened. Amalia closed the
door, came over to the shower, drew the curtain aside
and knelt in front of me. I hardly had time to shut off
the faucet so that she would not get splashed. I was
going to put my hands on her head but I was dripping
and would have spoiled her hairdo. I ended up hanging
onto the curtain rod and thinking: I must be losing my
mind but I find this woman enchanting.

My uncle was having his chocolate when I came into
the dining room.

"Did you boys get drunk?" he asked.

"A little."

"Such luck! What happened? Did you sell?"

"No."

"You did the right thing. It wouldn't be to your advantage."

"Didn't you tell me yesterday that it would be to
my advantage and that no matter what my cousins gave
for my share I would come out ahead of the game?"

"As a matter of fact, that is what I said. But what
place have you been to where I am known for always
telling the truth?"

I didn't know what to say to that. I stood there looking at him, trying to figure out if he was pulling my
leg. He said to me, "Fernando will be around today to
take you to The Yoke so you can see what you want
to charge for the survey."

I thought: Is that what is in store for me . . . to be
hanging around waiting for an inheritance and fabri-
cating topographical surveys?

Lucero came into the dining room wearing blue jeans,

a white T-shirt, and no brassière. I guess my uncle and I must have looked at her with the same expression on our faces.

Then Amalia brought in the medicine, and while she and my uncle were discussing something or other, Lucero came over to me and said in a very natural way, "I tried to get into your room last night, but couldn't."

The more complex my situation became, the guiltier I felt and the more anxious I was to get the money to the Chamuca and appease my conscience. For that reason, when I came out of the house and saw Fernando waiting for me out in the street, leaning against the Land Rover, I preferred to commit an indiscretion rather than let another day go by without sending her money.

"I have to send a wire before we leave for The Yoke," I told him.

Fernando accompanied me to the telegraph office. Not only did he come in with me, but he stood beside me as I wrote the Chamuca's name, her address in Jerez, the amount I was sending—a thousand pesos—in letters and numerals, and the five-word message included gratis in the price, which said: *See you Saturday. Love you.*

"Your girlfriend?" asked Fernando, who had been peeping.

"No, a moneylender I owe a thousand pesos."

"I thought I saw you write 'love you.' "

" 'I owe you' is what I wrote, not 'love you,' " I said, turning the form over.

Fernando walked on ahead of me and when we came to the Land Rover he got behind the wheel, saying, "I'll drive. I know the road better than you do."

We got stuck anyway, trying to cross the dry bed of the Bronco River. Fernando being at the wheel, I had

to get out and push. Fifteen meters away, three farmhands were shovelling sand into a truck. Instead of
giving us a hand, they stopped working to watch me
turn purple with my exertions. The spectacle struck
one of them as very funny, and he started to laugh.
When the car was finally out and on solid ground, I
turned to the farmhands and said, "Would the three of
you do me a favor and each go fuck his mother?"

They didn't answer or move. I walked over to the
Land Rover and climbed in. Fernando got out of the
other side and went over to them. "Boys," he said,
"keep it in mind that the person who insulted you was
in my car, but it wasn't me. I have never spoken disre-
spectfully to you."

When Fernando got back into the car and started it,
I said to him, "Tell me something, Fernando. Was I
right or wrong in telling those three off?"

"You were right," he answered, "but you have to
remember that you're here one day and gone the next.
I live here and don't want one of them taking a shot
at me out of resentment for what you said. That's the
reason I tried to smooth it over."

Relations between Fernando and me remained pretty
well fouled up after this exchange, which is why I replied to his next statement the way I did.

He said, "My brothers want me to ask you what we
were going to ask you last night before we got side-
tracked. How much do you want for your share of the
inheritance?"

"Before I sell you my share, I'd sooner give it away
to the Sisters of the Divine Word."

He stared at me with the same expression as the
three farmhands when I suggested what they could do
to their mothers. I immediately regretted having answered him as I did and was to be even sorrier later
on. If my cousins had given me money then and I had

gone and picked up the Chamuca and left with her for Half Moon Beach, a lot of misfortune could have been avoided.

That afternoon in the trunk room I drew up the configuration. Lucero arrived at five-thirty, and very quietly, without even saying hello, sat down at her easel and began to draw various versions of what I assumed was going to be a portrait of me. I pretended not to notice what she was doing and did my best to avoid seeing the outcome. By the time I finished transferring the portion of the polygonation I had begun to the paper, my hands were trembling. My excitement was nearly unbearable. I took the plan off the table, rolled it up carefully, and put it aside with the field book, after which I took another sheet of drawing paper and spread it out on the table. Lucero continued sketching, looking at me from time to time, biting her lower lip. I went to the door, closed it, and threw the bolt to keep Poison out. I then went and stood behind Lucero, who continued sketching, put my hands on her shoulders, and said, "Come on."

She stood up, followed me to the center of the room, and let me take off her sandals, trousers, panties, and T-shirt.

"Sit here," I said, pointing to the clean paper I had just spread over the table. "Now raise your legs and put them over my shoulders."

She obeyed. Everything worked out so well that I didn't even care when her orgasm made her squeeze her legs together so violently that I was nearly strangled. She mooed just like Amalia.

(SUNDAY MORNING)
Going to the Bagre River with "The Gringo" to shoot

at agachonas seems to me the stupidest possible way there can be to waste a Sunday morning. (The agachona is an aquatic bird that feeds on mosquitoes, tastes of swamp, and is considered a delicacy in the state of Plan de Abajo. Its name comes from the fact that when it feels that it is being attacked, it ducks, submerging in the water, throwing the hunter off his aim and making him miss.)

I sit on a stone among the reeds with the shotgun "The Gringo" has lent me in my hand. The river stretches before me and is about twenty meters wide at this point. The water, which has no current, looks like coffee with milk. "The Gringo's" theory is that the agachonas will appear at the opposite bank between the cattails and the willows. He is sitting on another stone, twenty meters upstream, almost hidden by the reeds. His arm is still bandaged but not in a sling. I hope it is well enough for him to shoot the rifle he is using, a 7mm automatic. It seems absolutely idiotic to me that he should be shooting agachonas with a rifle powerful enough to knock down a deer. I hope "The Gringo" will not fire before I do because I am sure he will miss and scare off the agachonas, which one hits either on the first shot or not at all.

I am hungry. "The Gringo" came by to pick me up before I was even finished dressing, so I had no time for breakfast. I am also sweating, because the Santa Marta poncho, which felt very comfortable a little while ago, makes me infernally hot now that the sun is up. I take it off, put it on the rock, and sit down on it.

The agachonas appear. There are four of them and they are swimming upstream, that is, they will be passing by me before they reach "The Gringo," which is an advantage. Now I notice that there is a dead tree-trunk in the water between the agachonas and me that stands in my way. For that reason, I cautiously get to my feet and take up a position about five meters downstream where the reeds are thickest. The agachonas, busy eating mosquitoes, have not noticed me. Poor little agachonas! I raise my shotgun and fire. Practically simultaneously, I hear the report of "The Gringo's" gun. The damn fool has ripped off a burst of five shots with his automatic rifle. Two of the agachonas are kicking their feet and the other two have ducked. In the excitement of the moment, I step into the water, getting my only trousers wet, and wade over to retrieve the bag. As I slog my way back to get out of the reeds, I notice that the two birds I am carrying have wounds made by shotgun pellets, which means that I killed them.

When I come out of the reeds I spot "The Gringo" on the path, his back to me. He jumps when he hears my footsteps, turns around, and sees me.

"Where were you?" he asks.

I tell him where. He is furious.

"You should have told me you were going to change your position. There could have been an accident."

When I pick up the Santa Marta poncho I had left on the rock, I notice three round holes in it. I say nothing.

Lucero baked the agachonas in a flaky pastry dough. She seasoned them so heavily that they didn't really taste bad to me. I said they were delicious, but to tell the truth I would have preferred to eat practically anything else. My uncle ate more than half the pie, washed down with the wine Amalia allowed him to have on Sundays. He turned to me and asked slyly, just to annoy "The Gringo," "And what was Jim doing while you were shooting agachonas?"

"The Gringo" pursed his lips and pressed them tightly

together, as though someone were trying to force a chickpea into his mouth.

That afternoon Lucero went out and I was able to work uninterruptedly in the trunk room for a good long while. The light was beginning to fade when the door opened and Amalia entered.

"Come with me," she beckoned. "I want to show you something absolutely divine."

I followed her, feeling the excitement her presence always aroused in me. The heels on the shoes she uses, for example, which are high and spiked—I am sure she could make a hole in one's skull with a blow from one of them—twist and slip as she crosses the kitchen patio, which is paved with cobblestones. They seem thoroughly ridiculous to me. Her legs, however, are hairy but very shapely, and they arouse a mixed feeling in me of repulsion and lascivious attraction. On the other hand, she makes remarks so grotesque that I feel tenderness toward her. For example, that afternoon, for some reason, I asked her, "What made you marry 'The Gringo'?"

Her answer was, "Because I've always liked everything American."

I hate myself because these idiocies awaken feelings of tenderness in me, and my not daring to tell her they are idiocies makes me hate myself even more. That is, I cannot accept Amalia as my equal, nor can I reject her.

She led me to the first door off the corridor, which is always kept locked, and opened it with a key she was carrying in her hand. We went into the parlor, which was in semidarkness because the shutters were closed.

"Look," she said, and turned on the switch.

What she wanted me to see was the chandelier.

It was a cut-glass chandelier with twelve lights that

my aunt Leonor would never turn on because, according to her, it used too much current.

"It's very large," I said.

"When I see it all lighted up I feel like I am in a fairy tale," Amalia said.

Then she turned off the light and locked the door, and we made love on the floor.

"Will you come to my room tonight?" she asked me two hours later as she was setting bottles on the tray to carry into the office.

"I don't think I'll be able to," I said. "I still have a lot of work to finish."

I spent the night with Lucero.

8

"I am going to pass a few days away from your house," I told my uncle at breakfast.

"Where are you going?"

"To live near the mine."

"What is that going to get you?"

"I think I'll be able to work better. I am wasting too much time going back and forth."

"That's all very well, but what about me?" asked my uncle. "Who am I going to drink cognac with after supper?"

He was really annoyed.

When I left the house, my cousins were outside waiting for me.

"Come to the Casino with us," Alfonso said. "We must talk to you."

We walked along in silence, Fernando and Gerardo ahead, Alfonso and I behind. Alfonso carried a briefcase. Everybody we passed in the street greeted us. Paco of the Casino opened the game room and had one of the waiters bring us coffee with milk, which was all that was available that early in the morning.

As we were stirring our coffee, Alfonso took the floor. "Fernando says you said you would sooner turn your share over to the Sisters of Saint Vincent . . ."

". . . of the Divine Word," corrected Fernando.

". : . of the Divine Word than sell it to us, your cousins, who were interested in buying it from you."

"Provided the asking price was reasonable," Gerardo amended.

I was going to say that I had changed my mind and decided to sell, but my cousins did not give me a chance.

"Your attitude is causing us problems," said Fernando.

"And we consider it very selfish," said Gerardo.

"But we have decided to go along with it," said Fernando, "and make you another proposition you might find more interesting."

It was as follows: Since my uncle Ramón's only heirs were the four of us seated at that table, plus Amalia, there was a very simple approach to all the uncertainties. It would be sufficient for the five of us to sign an agreement, legalized by a notary, in which we would declare our intention of totalling all the assets left us by my uncle Ramón in his will and, upon his death, dividing the whole five ways.

"In that manner," Alfonso finished saying, "we would have the assurance that when my uncle is, unfortunately, no longer with us, each of the signatories will come into assets worth three and a half million pesos, in round numbers. How does that strike you?"

I would have preferred to have the money in my hand, but I said, "Sounds fine." My cousins were very pleased at my response. Alfonso opened his briefcase and took out some papers. There were six copies of the agreement he had just prepared. I noted that one of the parties had already signed. I read the name "Amalia Tarragona de Henry" in the handwriting of a backward convent-school pupil. I don't know why it should have aroused a feeling of tenderness in me rather than the indignation I might have felt at seeing that signature in green ink—inasmuch as I realized that Amalia had probably signed the agreement before she led me to see the chandelier, and had said nothing to me about it. I took out my pen and signed each page and at the end of the six copies of the document. My cousins did the same.

"One copy for each of us," Alfonso explained, "and one for Zorrilla, who will register the document today."

I put my copy in my pocket, said goodbye to my cousins, and went to the men's room. I was passing water when Paco of the Casino came over and stood at the next urinal.

"You are the heir," he said to me.

"What do you mean, the heir?"

"Yes. Ramón did it all in secret but I am going around town betting that you are the heir. Would you like to take a thousand pesos?"

"Thanks very much, no."

On the road to The Cauldron, I thought to myself: I come from up in the hills, my dad was a loser, everybody calls me El Negro, the one member of my family who got rich started out as a whore, and I lost fourteen million pesos just by signing my name. To say that life has handed me a royal screwing would be putting it mildly.

When I got back to the house in the afternoon, as Zenaida opened the door, she said to me, beaming, "The señora has arrived."

I didn't even dare ask her whose señora. I felt like a tightrope walker doing pirouettes on a wire who suddenly finds that he has lost his balance and is plunging headlong to the floor.

I saw the following scene in the corridor: My uncle in his wheelchair and "The Gringo" in a rocking chair, turned in different directions but their eyes converging on the same point—the Chamuca's dark-skinned legs. She was sitting in one of the leather armchairs, wearing a yellow dress I had not seen before, which I learned later she had bought with part of the thousand pesos I had sent her, like an idiot, two days before.

The Chamuca did not turn around to look at me because her attention was fixed on my uncle, who was telling the hyena joke again. Amalia and Lucero, sitting in the wicker settee—the first time I had ever seen them together—on the contrary were not looking at the Chamuca's legs, nor at my uncle, but at me, as I approached the group. I must say, that corridor had never seemed so long to me before.

When my uncle came to the punchline, the Chamuca and "The Gringo" burst out laughing, I tried to smile, and Amalia and Lucero kept looking at me grimly. When she had stopped laughing the Chamuca stood up, came over to me, and kissed me on the lips. As we separated, my uncle said, "You made two serious mistakes, Marcos. The first was not to have brought your wife to the house from the beginning, and the second was not being here in time to receive her. My congratulations, she's charming."

I didn't dare look at either Lucero or Amalia. I said to the Chamuca, "I'm happy you came, but I wasn't expecting you."

"I couldn't wait anymore to see you."

"Amalia," said my uncle, "have the other bed in the twins' room made up."

Amalia stood up and, as she went by, said to me in a whisper, "You're heartless!"

It was a dreadful afternoon. Amalia again changed the order in which she passed out the plates at the dinner table. I was served last. When the meal was over my uncle wanted to show the Chamuca through the house, and we had to push him as far as the hen coops. At a moment when I was alone with Lucero, I asked, "Are you angry?"

"No," she replied, "sad."

In the afternoon, the three women sat in the corridor talking about clothes and the advantages of living in a small town. Then we drove in two cars to Rabbit Hill to see the sunset. In the evening my cousins arrived for supper to meet the Chamuca. As we sat around the table after eating, she played a guitar my uncle ordered to be brought out of a wardrobe, and sang "Guajira Patrol." At night, I tried to make love to her but couldn't.

The next day the Chamuca and I went to live in the hotel at The Cauldron.

(THURSDAY, APRIL 24)

My finished work is in front of me on the hotel ping-pong table. The configuration plan, which seems to be quite accurate, is 1.20 meters wide and does not coincide with the aerial map of the region. The Hill Without a Name, for example, looks circular on the map but is oval on the plan I drew, which looks more elegant and is perhaps even closer to the actual topography— none of which is of the slightest importance. There are twenty sheets of graph paper under the general heading of "Costs and Profitability Study," filled with calculations whose meaning I understand but which would be too complicated and completely pointless to explain here. At the end of the report there are five typewritten pages entitled "Conclusions and Recommendations," in which I show incontrovertibly that, although very rich, the mine would be unprofitable to operate on a small scale.

It is 8:00 P.M.; there are mosquitoes on the veranda where I have been working continuously for the last three days. There being no other guests but us, doña Petra, who is in charge of the hotel, permitted me to use the ping-pong table. We are leaving for Muérdago in the Land Rover in a few minutes. While the Chamuca waits in the town square there, I will take the report to my uncle, who, under the terms of the contract, has to pay me forty thousand pesos. Tomorrow, the Chamuca and I will be off to the Aurora Hotel on Half Moon Beach, where we have reservations.

PART TWO

9

The only thing out of the ordinary that ever happened in my life is what I am now going to tell about. After fifty years of being a druggist, I became a detective. I can't say I made a success of this new line of work, but I did a better job than the professionals who were involved in the case I had to solve.

I think it would be a good idea to begin by pointing out that, indirectly, I was the cause of the crimes I later had to investigate. If, on the night I was closing up the drugstore when Marcos González passed by and greeted me and I recognized him, I had said, as some people do, "Nice seeing you, good night, and good luck," it's possible that he would have gone his way and no misfortunes would have occurred. However, that's not how it happened, because I took a liking to Marcos the moment I saw him since he so much resembled his aunt Leonor Alcántara, one of the people I most admired and respected in my life. Besides being tired that night, he wore a beard, a poncho, and very strange-looking shoes, which, as he told me later, are called "Argentine boots." In any case he looked like Leonor, and I took a shine to the boy. When he told me he had been to Ramón's house and that Amalia wouldn't let him in, I didn't hesitate to invite him to spend the night at my house. That was how I reacted on the spur of the moment, and I consider I did the right thing, because to have had an inkling of the consequences that were to follow one would have had to be a crystal-gazer. When he told me the story of the mine, I believed it implicitly. Not only did I trust him, but it seemed to me that the business he was proposing would be a very good thing for Ramón. The following day I took him to his uncle's house, stood up for him, and even witnessed the agreement the two of them signed. I did all that and I don't regret it. If there turned out to be fatal consequences, it couldn't be helped.

On the day after the uncle and nephew met, I noticed that my essence of Sparta was low. It is a basic ingredient in any pharmacy and can only be obtained from Dr. Ballesteros in Cuévano. I had no choice but to make the trip to the capital of my state. I had concluded my errand and left Dr. Ballesteros's pharmacy with the essence of Sparta in my pocket when I saw Marcos. My first impulse was to call out to him, but he was some distance away and seemed to be in a hurry. He came out of the Flor de Cuévano, crossed Constitution Square, threw something into a trash can and went off to the left, in the direction of Triumph of Bustos Street.

I guess something about his behavior gave me a bad impression, because it led me to do something I wouldn't normally do. I wanted to see what Marcos had thrown in the trash. Fortunately it was an open receptacle with no cover to push aside, which would have made it demeaning. There were five Mexico City newspapers of the same day in the can.

As I walked toward the bus depot, I asked myself what reason he could have had to buy five different papers of the same day. Either he was looking for a job, he wanted to buy a house, or he was waiting for a piece of news that interested him. When I got to the depot, I bought copies of *Excélsior*, *El Universal*, *La Prensa*, *El Sol de México*, and *El Heraldo*. I read them on the bus during the trip back to Muérdago, trying to locate an item that might have interested Marcos. I disregarded all international news, the society pages, and the editorial sections, and was left with: a bankers' convention being held in Acapulco; a former government official accused of stealing 110 million pesos; a woman who had stabbed her landlady; another woman who had tortured her son; and, on page 18 of *Excélsior*, a piece about terrorists arrested the day before by the police, in which a fugitive with the alias "El Negro" was mentioned.

I cut out this last item with my penknife, and when I got off the bus in Muérdago I did what I had seen Marcos do in Cuévano—I threw all five newspapers into the nearest trash can.

It was ten minutes after three. I was hungry and knew that my wife would be expecting me, but instead of going straight home I went to Ramón's house, hoping to have a word with him before he took his siesta. At that moment, I must admit, I had no idea what I was going to tell him, but I did feel I had to talk to him about Marcos. When the two of us were shut up in his office, he asked me a question that took me by surprise. "Doesn't that story Marcos told us about the beryllium mine sound like hokum to you?" he said.

"What makes you say that?"

"Because I found out this morning that Marcos had sixty-one pesos in his pocket."

"So what?"

"What do you mean 'so what?' Here he is offering me a business deal that will run into the millions and I agree to his doing a job for which he is going to charge me a fifty-thousand-peso fee, but all he has in his pocket is sixty-one pesos. The natural thing for him to have said would have been, 'Uncle, I'm flat. Give me five thousand on account.' His not asking for an advance tells me there's something fishy about what he is proposing and he doesn't want to call undue attention to himself because he is afraid I might find out he's up to some shenanigans.''

Even though my reason for coming to see Ramón had been to put him on the alert, when I found that he had already gotten suspicious I felt he was being unfair.

"It's also possible that he was simply embarrassed to ask you for money," I said.

He was as indecisive about Marcos as I was. He said, "Sure, it could have been that. I thought the same thing. That's why I gave him a thousand pesos this morning."

"You gave him a thousand pesos?"

"Which I never expect to see again. Not only that, but I had Fernando lend him the Land Rover."

"And now you feel you won't get anything back?"

"I'm convinced of it. I wasn't very smart, because he could have taken Alfonso's Galaxy, which is a much more expensive car but has the big advantage of not belonging to me. I don't know what's gotten into me at my age that's making me generous."

"For somebody on the run," I said, "Marcos hasn't gone very far. I saw him in Cuévano only a little while ago."

This was obviously reassuring news. Nevertheless, Ramón said to me, "Bet you a thousand pesos I never see the other thousand, nor Marcos, nor the Land Rover again."

I took the bet thinking I was going to lose. I said nothing about having seen Marcos throwing the newspapers into the trash, but I did ask Ramón, "Say, what was the nickname Marcos's cousins used to call him? 'El Negro' or something like that?"

"His cousins and everybody else who knew him called him 'El Negro' for the simple reason that he's black."

I said goodbye and was on my way out when Ramón

said to me, "Tell Zenaida that if Marcos comes back here to serve him whatever he wants to eat."

That same afternoon, Zenaida arrived at the drugstore and handed me one of the little folded notes Ramón used to communicate with me. He had stopped telephoning me since Amalia and Lucero had come to live in his house, convinced that Amalia listened in on his conversations over the telephone in her bedroom. The message said, "The birdie is back and has brought the samples. Come to the house and bring the encyclopedia to see if the stones are really cryolite."

As usual Ramón didn't say "please" and, as usual, I obeyed immediately. I left the clerk in charge of the pharmacy and went to my friend's house with two volumes of the Encyclopedia of Science and Art. I found him in his office, examining the stones on the desk.

"Close the door," he said, and after I had done so he continued, "and look up the word 'cryolite.'" Then, in a different tone of voice, he said, "Bet you a hundred pesos these stones are not cryolite."

I opened one of the volumes, found the word "cryolite," looked at the illustration, compared it with the stones on the desk, and said, "You owe me one thousand one hundred pesos."

"Why one thousand one hundred?"

"Because Marcos came back and because the stones are cryolite."

"Just a minute. Marcos came back and brought the Land Rover, but I haven't seen the thousand pesos I gave him this morning. So I don't win or lose. As far as these stones looking like the illustration goes, I agree."

He took out a hundred-peso note and gave it to me. It was the only time I ever saw Ramón pay off a bet. I realized that he was happy Marcos had returned.

"I want you to go to Cuévano tomorrow," he said to me, "and take these samples to the laboratory to see if it's true that they have as high a metal content as the boy claims."

Having to go to Cuévano again the next day was a nuisance, but Ramón seemed so enthusiastic about the mine and so interested that I promised to do as he wished.

"I did another stupid thing," he confessed.

"What now?"

"I gave Marcos nine thousand pesos more."

"That wasn't in the agreement."

"I know. And that's not all. Not only did I give him nine thousand pesos I wasn't obliged to, but I told him he could have the Land Rover for as long as he needed it. And, what's even worse, I promised to give Marcos a letter to engineer Requena asking him to lend him surveying instruments he says he needs. This means that although he did come back today, he might disappear tomorrow, and I'm out ten thousand pesos, a car in very good condition, and surveying instruments worth a fortune."

"If you distrust him so much why are you doing all this for him?"

He did not look me in the eye as he answered, "I guess it's because he reminds me of Leonor."

There wasn't anything I could say to that because I had the same weakness regarding Marcos.

Ramón then said, "I am going to make out my will tomorrow."

"Good idea," I told him. "Now, while you are in your right mind."

I thought he was going to tell me what he was putting in his will. I waited, but he said nothing more, so I stood up and put the stones in the sack.

"I have to go back to the drugstore," I said.

He said goodbye, and not another word about his will.

The next day, when I was in Cuévano, I went to see Carlitos Inastrillas, who had been a schoolmate of mine and is now director of the Mining Registry. I found him looking very peaked, but he received me cordially. He asked what miracle had brought me to his office.

"I want you to find out for me if there is a mine in this state called the Covadonga."

Carlitos sent for the head of archives. Never have I received such efficient and rapid service from a couple of bureaucrats. The head of archives told us that the Covadonga did exist and that a "nonregistration certificate" had been issued for it that very day.

"The 'nonregistration certificate,'" Carlitos explained to me while the head of archives went for the file, "means that the mine has not been claimed or that the previous claim has expired and it is open to be worked once more."

When Carlitos had the file in front of him and the head of archives had left, he read to me: "The Covadonga is in the township of Las Tuzas on lands of the former hacienda The Cauldron."

Of everything he might have told me, this was the most reassuring. Not only did the Covadonga actually exist, but it was situated on lands close to where Marcos and his family had been born and had lived. Furthermore, Marcos had taken the official steps as he had promised, having applied for and been issued the "nonregistration certificate."

"It was operated," Carlitos went on reading, "for the extraction of manganese ore."

If I had happened to mention the word cryolite at that moment, Carlitos would have explained to me that beryllium is never found where there is manganese. I said nothing, and did not learn about this peculiarity of mines until it was too late.

The results of the ore assay I had ordered that morning were satisfactory. The figure on one of the stones was .12 and on the other four it was .11. Higher, in both cases, than the .08 Marcos had initially estimated. I put the envelope with the results in my pocket, and was taking out my wallet to pay for the analysis when the technician said to me, "If you ever bring in ore from two different sites again, I suggest you separate the samples so as to avoid confusion."

It wasn't clear to me what he meant. He went on to say, "In this case, it doesn't make any difference because the ore samples from the two mines assayed have almost the same content, but that is unusual."

I went through the motions of counting and recounting the money, and then I asked him, "You mean you can tell just by looking at the samples I brought in that they came from two different mines?"

"No, not with the naked eye, but when I looked at them through the microscope there was no doubt about it, because the crystallizations were quite different."

When I left the university, I remained standing at Sun Street, looking around without seeing the passersby. I was sure I had not heard Marcos speak in the plural. He had not said either "mines" or cryolite "deposits." Why, then, did the samples he had brought Ramón come from different places? Was this irregularity another sign of bad faith?

When I saw Ramón again, I gave him only the good news. I told him that the Covadonga did exist, that it was located in The Cauldron, and that the results of the assay were more than satisfactory. He was happy because Marcos had returned, and what I told him put him in even better spirits.

"I'm beginning to think Marcos is on the level. Could it be that I'm getting into my dotage?"

I was going to tell him that Marcos had bought five newspapers of the same day, that he had thrown them into the trash can after reading them, that an individual with the nickname of "El Negro" was wanted by the police, that the cryolite samples I had taken for testing came from two different mines, and so forth. But I decided it would be easier to keep my mouth shut, and that's what I did.

The following day, I was sitting on a bench in the square when Paco of the Casino came over to me and said, "I'll lay you a thousand pesos that the new nephew who just arrived from Mexico will be Ramón's sole heir."

Two bootblacks and a group of girls around the neighboring bench overheard him.

"Not so loud," I said to him, "Ramón's will is supposed to be a secret."

"I haven't said a thing. All I'm doing is making a bet. Do you take it or not?"

I went to Ramón and told him what Paco was going around betting on.

"I wonder if he didn't manage some way to see what you wrote."

Ramón let out a guffaw but did not tell me what was in the will. I was so annoyed at this lack of confidence in me that I kept away from him for several days. However, I did have news of the family. On Monday, when I sat down at the table for supper, Jacinta said to me, "Zenaida says that Marcos's wife has arrived."

"What wife? Marcos isn't married."

"Zenaida says she is young and very tall and has dark eyes."

With that, I now felt Marcos had gone too far. I decided he was not trustworthy.

The following night, Jacinta said to me, "Zenaida

says that Marcos and his wife went to live in a mine."

On Thursday afternoon, Zenaida came to the drugstore with another of Ramón's notes which said: "Come right away." Being annoyed with Ramón, I killed time and took half an hour in getting there.

"What took you so long?" he asked when we had sat down together in the corridor.

He was about as restless as a paralytic can get.

"I thought you were having your siesta," I said, to excuse myself.

"What makes you think I could be taking a siesta when I've been waiting for Marcos since this morning?"

He told me that Marcos had promised to bring him the costs and profitability study that morning.

"I had a check for forty thousand pesos made out and ready to give him, but he hasn't shown up."

"He could still get here."

"I don't think so. I think that when he left here with his wife to go and live at the mine, as he said, he had no intention of coming back. He is being very stupid, because if he'd stayed around for six months or so, I would have made a well-off man of him, maybe a millionaire. But all he wanted was to steal a car from me and ten thousand pesos."

Despite my being convinced that Ramón was right, that Marcos had disappeared and we would never see him again, I tried to make him accept the possibility that Marcos might have been delayed in finishing his work or had a mishap on the highway. He continued to be uneasy and I finally said to him, "I promise you that tomorrow I'll go find Marcos and bring him here to you."

It was seven o'clock when I said goodnight to Ramón.

I decided to get an early start. The taxi picked me up at six o'clock, and at six-thirty we were approaching the sign that says "THE CAULDRON. HOTEL AND BATHS. 10 KILOMETERS." A little further on, the car had to stop to let a drove of burros go by. I lowered my window and said to the drover, "There's an old mine around here somewhere, isn't there?"

"Keep going straight ahead until you come to the big mud puddle, then follow the road that goes around the side where the sun sets."

We followed his directions and came to a place where there was, in fact, an old mine. Something came over me, just as it had several other times in the last few days. I knew there had to be an old mine near The Cauldron, but even so I felt that the fact of actually seeing it proved that Marcos was telling the truth. I realize that this was nonsense on my part, but that's what I felt.

I got out of the car and went to look at a ruined house. Marcos couldn't be living there, I thought, and with his wife it seemed even less likely. The roofs were all caved in, but somebody had set up a wall made of stones in one of the windows, and there were traces of country people on the ground: peanut shells and sugar-cane pulp. I went back to the car and said to the driver, "Take me to the hotel."

The hotel had changed greatly since the last time I was there, forty years ago. It even had a sign that said LADIES BAR. The driver parked under some mesquite trees. I went in and walked through the lobby to the desk. There was nobody around. For that reason, it seemed a natural thing for me to open the register that lay on the counter. I turned the pages until I came to the entries of the last few days. Just as I suspected, Marcos's name was not there. The last names listed were "Angel Valdés and señora." They had arrived on Tuesday, that is, the day Marcos had left Muérdago.

A door creaked at the end of the hall, almost making me slam the book shut. A woman in slippers appeared and shuffled slowly toward me, looking at me distrustfully.

"What do you want?"

She had noticed the open register. I realized that I had interrupted her breakfast because there was a bit of tortilla in the corner of her mouth. I took a twenty-peso bill out of my wallet and put it on the counter. When the woman's eyes had come to rest on it I said, "I am looking for some people and would like your help in finding them."

She took her eyes off the bill, looked at the register, at me, and at the bill again.

"I don't know if I can help you, señor."

"He is dark and has curly hair. His wife, they tell me, is tall and has very pretty eyes."

"No. I haven't seen them."

I took out another twenty-peso bill and put it alongside the other one on the counter.

"He was wearing a Santa Marta poncho."

"Ah, now I know who you're talking about. It's the couple in 106."

I gave her the two bills before saying, "Please tell him that José Lara would like to talk to him."

"I can't do that, señor."

I took out another twenty-peso bill. Looking at it sadly, she said to me, "Because they left last night."

I didn't believe her and said, "Do you want these twenty pesos? I'll give them to you if you can show me that these people aren't here anymore. It is very urgent that I see them."

She went around the counter, opened a drawer, and showed me the receipted bill for Room 106. The account had been paid at 8:30 P.M. I gave the woman the bill I had in my hand.

It cost me another forty pesos to see Room 106, in which I found nothing of interest, and to carefully check

the extras that appeared on the bill. I was interested in
two phone calls, one to Ramón's house at 5:30 on the
afternoon of the previous day, that is, before I had gotten there. The other call had also been made the day
before to a number in the Ticomán area.

It cost me another twenty pesos to put those stubs
in my wallet.

"Now, will you connect me with Muérdago?" I said
to the woman, giving her my name and Ramón's number.

Amalia answered. I said, "It's José Lara, Amalia. Good
morning. I'd like a word with Ramón."

"My uncle Ramón died last night," she told me.

10

Ramón and I knew each other from the time we were children but we became friends when we went to college in Cuévano and lived in the same boarding house. At that time, Ramón was a thin young man who wore hard collars and worsted suits discarded by his brother "Handsome," to whom they had been handed down by don Enrique, their father, who was noted in Muérdago for being an elegant dresser but on the thrifty side. Every Monday he sent each of his children who were going to school in Cuévano a six-peso postal money order for their weekly allowance. That was more than enough for "Handsome," since he was a model young man, but to Ramón six pesos was a bagatelle. He thought up a business which had the advantage of requiring no astuteness, effort, or capital. Using his father as guarantor—without his father being aware of it—he obtained premises that he named The Warehouse. Next, on the basis of nothing but promises, he secured the services of a very honest man who became the manager. Ramón was the "agent." He "accepted" on commission anything and everything at The Warehouse that did not spoil and that was needed by everybody, from coal and wood to wax candles. Ramón did nothing outside of going to The Warehouse daily to divide up the commissions with the manager.

Ramón, thanks to The Warehouse, and I, thanks to Ramón's generosity, lived our student years in comfort.

Weekdays, after classes, we got together with friends at The Classroom, a bar on Sun Street, opposite the university. Each time Ramón paid for a round, he would get the money back later playing Twenty-one. In the evenings we played billiards, and on Saturdays we invariably went to señora Aurelia's place in the Malaquitas alley, which was the only whorehouse in Cuévano for the upper crust. On Sundays, however, we attended eleven o'clock Mass at the parish church and then played tennis at Dr. Miranda's house, until the doctor invited us to dinner. The three Miranda daughters fell in love with Ramón and he, in time, became the beau of the oldest daughter, Margarita.

Supposedly we were studying law, but we rarely went to class, preferring, in addition to the pastimes mentioned, to go swimming in the Tepozanes reservoir, to fight the cows in the Palito corral, or simply to sit around in Constitution Square watching the people go by. We were there one day when "Handsome" came over to us and said to Ramón, "You have dragged the family name through the mud."

When Ramón realized that what "Handsome" was referring to was that he should have been attending his Roman law class at that hour, he burst out laughing.

As was to be expected, we flunked out in our third year and returned to Muérdago, our hometown. Ramón took over the management of The Yoke hacienda—which belonged to his father—and I went to work in La Fe drugstore, which belonged to my mother. Although we didn't have as much in the way of amusement as we had had when we were students, Ramón and I would see each other daily. We became members of the Casino and played billiards every afternoon. On Saturdays at five o'clock sharp we would be on the train to Cuévano. When we arrived there we would take a room at the Palace Hotel. That night we would visit señora Aurelia's place and on Sunday we attended eleven o'clock Mass and played tennis at the Miranda house until the doctor invited us to lunch. Margarita produced wonders in the kitchen every Sunday, and every Sunday on the train back to Muérdago Ramón would say to me, looking through the window at the hills in the evening twilight, "I love Margarita very much and I am going to marry her, but not right away."

Three years went by.

One Saturday night, doña Aurelia received us with special enthusiasm. "I have something that could have been made to order for you boys." When we wanted to know what it was, she explained, "It's a girl who just arrived from the hot country."

We accepted this news with certain reservations inasmuch as doña Aurelia had in the past come up with an assortment of frights. But that night she parted the strings of beads hanging in the doorway that opened off the foyer and called in a tall, well-built girl who, despite the dress she was wearing, looked very elegant. She was a mulatta with honey-colored eyes. Sitting at the table with us and doña Aurelia, she spoke little, keeping her eyes cast down, said her name was Estela, and that she was not from the tropical coast but had been born at The Cauldron—a farm way up in the hills known for its mineral springs. Doña Aurelia went on making conversation until Ramón interrupted her to ask me, "Are you going with her or am I?"

We tossed a coin for Estela and Ramón won.

When I left señora Aurelia's place, I returned to the hotel and went to bed. It was getting light when I woke up. Ramón was sitting on his bed taking his shoes off. On seeing me awake, he said, "She's very nice."

Sunday began as usual. We attended Mass and played tennis, and Dr. Miranda invited us to lunch. Margarita prepared delights, and so on. However, as we walked toward the station carrying our suitcases, Ramón suddenly stopped and said to me, "Do me a favor. When you get to Muérdago, go to my house and explain to my mother that a classmate of ours died and I had to stay over for the wake. Tell her I'll be back tomorrow on the eight o'clock train."

I agreed to do it, he walked me to the station, and before saying goodbye we invented the deceased's name—Gonzalo Gonzaga. He crossed the little square near the station, almost at a run. Judging by the route he took, I realized he was heading straight for the Malaquitas alley.

And so began the most hectic period in Ramón's life. Besides the trips we made every Saturday, he spent two or three weekday nights in Cuévano, returning on the eight o'clock train to Muérdago, where a peon would be waiting for him at the station with horses to ride to The Yoke. This activity did not pass unnoticed. Inevitably rumors were started, and one of them would have to reach Dr. Miranda's ears. One Sunday he did not invite us to lunch. Margarita nearly fainted. We said goodbye to the family very politely and went to eat at the Palace Hotel. We sat in silence until the fruit paste and cheese they always served for dessert were in front of us, when Ramón said, "I know what I am going to do. I am going to bring her to live in Muérdago."

"Margarita?"

"No, Leonor."

"Who is Leonor?"

"Estela. Her name is Leonor Alcántara."

"Are you going to marry her?"

"No, I'm going to marry Margarita."

During the following days, I helped him look for a house in Muérdago. We found one near the brick works in the San José section that seemed suitable to Ramón.

"That section gets flooded in the rainy season," I warned him.

"That's true," he said, "but it has the advantage that nobody knows me there."

He bought the house, had it painted, and installed running water, which it did not have, and a toilet. I asked him why he did not have a hot water heater and bathtub put in while he was at it.

"It would be wasted," he told me, "because I am going to stay on in my own house and Leonor is used to bathing in a washtub."

After Leonor came to live in Muérdago, Ramón made fewer and fewer trips to Cuévano. One day he explained to me, "I love Margarita very much and one of these days I am going to marry her. The reason I don't go to Cuévano very often is that there are potholes in the tennis court."

I was there the day the engagement was broken off. After several weeks of not going to Cuévano, we made the effort and went one Sunday morning. On entering the church to attend eleven o'clock Mass, we saw a mining engineer, a widower with three children, sitting in one of the pews reading from the prayer book Margarita Miranda was holding in her hand. Ramón turned to me and said, "Frankly, I see no point in staying for the sermon."

We left the church during the offertory. Not only did we not play tennis at the Mirandas' again, but we never went to Mass again.

When don Enrique died, he left the house on Sonaja Street to "Handsome," who was married and had children. Ramón had to go and live with Leonor in the little house in the San José section that got flooded in August. After he had spent a number of years there, one day he said to me, "In a certain sense, my life has been a failure. I'm Jesus Christ's age and don't even have a bathroom yet."

He had to go clear across Muérdago to the Russian baths at the Casino.

Ramón never referred to Leonor by name but always spoke of her in the most indirect way possible. For example, he would say, "Shirts are ironed nicely at the house." Or, "They don't know how to prepare spaghetti."

One day when we were in Pedrones he had me pick out a very fine perfume. "You're a druggist, you ought to know about such things," he said, but he did not tell me who it was for. Later, I noticed from the calendar that the following day was Saint Leonor's Day.

I don't believe I saw Leonor more than three times during the first fifteen years she lived in Muérdago. The first occasion was on the street that goes up Owl Hill. There was a fruit stand there that had prickly pears, and she was leaning over picking out the good ones. I had slowed down as I walked up the alley to admire her shape, not realizing it was Leonor. I must have blushed, because when she noticed me it made her laugh. "Good morning, Pepe," she said as she went by me with her basket over her arm.

Another time, I urgently needed Ramón's signature on a note at an hour when I knew he would be with Leonor at the house in the San José section, and I went there to talk to him. Leonor opened the door and was pleased to see me. "Come this way," she said.

She spoke to me in the familiar form because that was how she had addressed me the day we met at señora Aurelia's. She had me sit down in the foyer and went to notify Ramón, who soon emerged in his shirtsleeves, looking very solemn.

As we were discussing the papers he was to sign, Leonor brought in a tray covered with a very white napkin upon which there was a bottle of mezcal, two glasses, and canapés of imported lobster. Ramón and I ate and drank, pretending to be completely absorbed in the documents, as though it were the waiter at the Casino who was serving us and we were accustomed to eating lobster every day.

The third time I saw her was one morning when she came into the drugstore and, without greeting me, said, "Ramón is very sick."

"What's wrong with him?"

"A pain here," she said, putting her hand on her belly.

We went with Canalejas to the little house in the San José section. Canalejas examined Ramón and diagnosed acute appendicitis. We took Ramón to Pedrones, which had the only modern hospital in the state of Plan de Abajo at that time. The superintendent was a nun and would not let Leonor in because when Ramón gave his personal data he had said he was single. Realizing the touchiness of the situation, Ramón said, "That's it, then. We'll get married."

They were married in the corridor outside the operating room. Canalejas and I were the witnesses at the civil wedding and the best men at the religious ceremony. The operation was a success and during his convalescence Ramón received the kind of attention from the sisters that was befitting a patient who was both a wealthy man and a repentant sinner. When he was discharged, he returned to the house in the San José section and carried on his life with Leonor as usual.

"I can't explain it," Ramón confessed one day when we were alone, "but being married feels more embarrassing to me than living in sin."

When the Land Reform came to Plan de Abajo, Ramón offered to buy "Handsome's" share of The Yoke, and "Handsome" sold it for twenty-three thousand pesos, thinking he had made a killing. However, as time went by and The Yoke was not divided up and distributed, "Handsome" took it badly and said that his brother had conspired with the government to buy up his inheritance for peanuts. The resentment and the upright life he led—he was one of the worst hypocrites I ever knew—put him into an early grave. Oddly enough for a person who never took a drink, he died of what Candalejas diagnosed as cirrhosis of the liver, and stranger still for one who was careful about money to the point of miserliness, he left nothing but debts when he died. Ramón helped the family by buying the house on Sonaja Street from them for fifteen thousand pesos, paid for the moving so that they would vacate promptly, and went to live there with Leonor, whom the decent folk of Muérdago knew as "the woman Ramón was keeping in the San José section." Zenaida was already working for them by that time.

Ramón removed all traces left in the house by "Handsome's" family—he made a bonfire with a Divine Countenance and some purple curtains—and restored it to the way it had been in the time of his parents. Those who were expecting Ramón to give a reception to present his wife to Muérdago society were left waiting, and the only ones ever invited to the house were Canalejas, Zorrilla, and me. The food was excellent, and Leonor only entered the dining room to supervise the serving.

One day when we were in the town square we saw Margarita Miranda passing by with her husband and stepchildren. Ramón said to me, "I owe my having been saved from that fate to doña Aurelia."

His happiness lasted until one morning when Leonor, who apparently had never even had a headache in her life, suddenly fell to the floor dead as she was setting the table.

11

"I was in the dining room, serving my uncle his chocolate," said Amalia, "when I heard a banging on the door."

Amalia, who had gained weight since she was last in mourning, wore a black dress that was too small for her. I had never seen her without makeup and stared at her in surprise. Without mascara, her eyes looked red and swollen, as though she had been weeping over Ramón's death, which was unlikely. We sat on uncomfortable chairs in the parlor and she told us, me and the others who had just arrived, what had happened during Ramón Tarragona's last hours. His body had been wrapped in a shroud by the women, my wife and Zenaida among them, and would be laid out in the bedroom until the casket was delivered, because Alfonso had not been able to get one in Muérdago elegant enough for Ramón's remains and had ordered the finest one available in Pedrones by telephone. The room was dark and, since it was rarely opened, smelled of musty brocades.

Amalia went on with her account. "I hope that's Marcos, I thought, because I knew my uncle had been waiting for him anxiously all day. 'I'll see who it is,' I said to my uncle, since Zenaida had gone out on an errand. When I stepped into the corridor, I saw that Lucero had opened the door and was talking to Marcos. 'Thank goodness you finally got here,' I said to him,

'My uncle has been expecting you since early this morning.' Marcos was carrying rolls of plans and a lot of papers. 'I wasn't able to finish the work until now,' he told me. I had him go right into the dining room. My uncle pushed his cup of chocolate aside. 'Finish your supper, uncle,' I said. 'Bother supper! Wheel me to my office,' he said. 'Have a glass of milk, at least,' I begged him. 'Send in the cognac bottle,' he ordered. That was the routine. After supper, my uncle and Marcos would go into his office to talk and Lucero or I would bring them a bottle of cognac for Marcos to drink and a bottle of mineral water for my uncle, because he was forbidden alcoholic beverages. My uncle's being so stubborn last night about not finishing his supper put me in a bad humor and so I fixed their tray for them and had Lucero take it to the office. When she came out Marcos shut the door behind her, and she and I sat down in the corridor without speaking. There were a lot of mosquitoes. It must have been ten o'clock when Zenaida came back. 'Aren't you going to have supper?' she asked us, and I answered, 'I guess so. Heat up something for us.' She fixed a little snack and we were eating it when we heard the door of the office open and close, then Marcos's footsteps. When he came to the dining-room door, he stopped there without coming in and said, 'Good night.' 'What do you mean, good night? Aren't you having supper with us?' I told him that there were lentils, which he likes very much. 'I'm in a big rush,' he said to us, 'I can't even stop for a minute.' He came into the dining room, gave us each a kiss, and left. Lucero and I went to the office to see if my uncle wanted anything. We found him writing. 'Would you like something, uncle?' I asked him. 'Not right now,' he said, 'but when I finish this letter I want Zenaida to put it in the mailbox tonight.' Lucero and I returned to the dining room and finished our supper. When we heard my uncle shouting 'Zenaida!' the three of us went to the office. The letter was in a sealed and stamped envelope. My uncle handed it to Zenaida and told her to go out and drop it in the mailbox. I didn't see to whom it was addressed. He also gave her a note to take to you, don Pepe."

"I never received it," I said.

Amalia went on. " 'Wouldn't you like your supper now?' I asked my uncle. 'No,' he said, 'I want to go to bed.' Zenaida left the house and Lucero and I helped him to bed. When I looked at him there in his bed, he seemed very tired. 'Do you feel all right?' I asked him. 'Very drowsy,' he answered. 'Sleep well,' I said to him. 'The same to you,' he answered. Then he looked at his watch and said, 'It's eleven-twenty, already.' I turned off the light and we left the room."

That morning at seven o'clock—Amalia went on to say—Zenaida brought him the cup of herb tea he usually drank before getting up. She knocked several times, but there was no answer and, finally realizing that something was wrong, she pushed open the door, which was ajar, and went into the bedroom. Ramón was dead in his bed and already stiff. Canalejas, who had made the prognosis of Ramón's death some time ago, wrote "infarct" as the cause of death in the certificate.

"Handsome's" sons were dressed in black and their wives were crying. "The Gringo" had put on a necktie. When Amalia finished her story, everybody kneeled and recited the rosary. Never had a rosary seemed so long to me. After the Five Mysteries, the Our Father, three Ave Marias, and the Salve were over, Amalia added a De Profundis and a special prayer for the peace of the souls of those who die in their sleep, and still another to the Virgin to intercede for those who have not received absolution, and then we prayed a litany— I am sure I heard Virgo Veneranda three times—which we were in the middle of when I felt a hand on my shoulder. It was Canalejas, who was standing beside me. He made a sign to me to follow him. I got up with some difficulty, not being used to kneeling, and followed him out of the room. He stopped in the doorway and said to me in a low voice, "I want you to have a look at the body and give me your opinion."

We were on our way through the corridor when I saw Lucero and Zenaida crossing the patio. Lucero held a coffee pot in her hand and Zenaida, who wore her shawl draped in the appropriate form for mourning, carried a tray of cups. When Lucero saw me, she put the coffee pot down on a table and came over to me, and we embraced. Lucero cried in my arms for a few moments and then stepped back, and I gave her my handkerchief. She dried her tears, smiled, picked up the coffee pot, and went on her way to the living room. Canalejas was waiting for me in the doorway of Ramón's bedroom. We went in together.

Ramón was laid out on his bed in a shroud. His skin had turned leaden white, the edge of a tooth showed between his lips, and his beard, which had not been shaved, formed a sort of silvery halo around his face. Then I noticed that tiny bluish circles had formed at the base of his lower lip. It was the classical sign of poisoning from an overdose of zafia water.

Arandula vertiginosa is the scientific name for the zafia. It is a plant with a white root similar to a turnip's, from which grow curly, dark-colored leaves that spread in circular form over the ground. The flower is purple, and so is the berry, which is about the size and shape of a chokecherry. The plant as a whole and each of its parts gives off a fetid odor. It is also called *nenepixtle* in the nahuatl language. It grows in the deep shade and at the edges of streams.

The pitted berry of the zafia plant, dried in the sun, is ground to a fine powder in a mortar and mixed in equal parts with a ten percent solution of tremic acid. The product obtained is called zafia water, one of the most versatile and effective medicines known, but one to be used with caution. One drop of zafia water in half a glass of water, taken after eating, relieves acidity; two drops taken at eleven o'clock stimulate the appetite; five drops act as a strong aphrodisiac; ten drops a day constitute an excellent heart tonic, and prolong life; thirty drops, however, taken all at once, endanger life, and two tablespoons of it will kill anybody. Another distinguishing characteristic of zafia water is that it is not habit-forming, which means that it can be discontinued suddenly without ill effects and, furthermore, that a patient who has been taking small quantities of zafia water over a long period does not become immunized against the effects of an overdose.

Canalejas and I looked at each other in silence for a moment before the recriminations began.

"It was your fault," I said to him.

"No," he said, "it was your fault."

"You were the one who prescribed zafia water for Ramón," I said.

"Of course I did, and it helped him a lot. But you were the one who prepared it. Couldn't you have made a mistake in the quantities?"

"I never make a mistake in my quantities, least of all when a medicine being taken by my best friend is involved."

"But you knew what a dangerous drug it is and how important the dosage is."

"Naturally I knew. That's why I keep your signed prescriptions on file in the pharmacy."

"You know perfectly well, Pepe, that the only pharmacist in Muérdago who knows how to prepare a zafia water is you. The rest of them are all a bunch of medicine men."

"And I know that the only physician who prescribes it is you. The others are all witch doctors."

"True enough. So you realize that we are in the same boat. Ramón is dead and it looks as though we killed him between us. Would you mind telling me what we do now?"

"I can't tell you a damn thing," I answered, "because since the minute we walked into this room, you've done nothing but nag the ass off me till I can't even think!"

Fortunately that shut him up, and the two of us stared in silence at the blue circles that were becoming more and more pronounced at the bottom of Ramón's lower lip.

Finally, I said to him, "I made up the last zafia water prescription last Tuesday, which means the bottle was full. No more than two doses could have been taken from it since then, that is, twenty drops. So it should be nearly full."

That was my first deduction.

Canalejas and I left the room and, as though to make up for the bad blood that had nearly come up between us, we took each other by the arm as we walked through the corridor. The funeral wreaths had begun to arrive, as well as some mourners—all people Ramón would not have wanted to see. In the living room, we took Amalia aside as circumspectly as possible and Canalejas said to her, "Listen, Amalia, Ramón was taking a medicine every morning. Do you remember where it was kept?"

"Naturally, I remember. I prepared it for him."

She took us to the office, pushed up the lid of the desk, opened one of the small drawers inside, and took out the little blue bottle of zafia water. Amalia stood staring at it in disbelief. "Yesterday norning it was nearly full," she exclaimed.

As was to have been expected, the little blue bottle of zafia water was empty. However, I noticed something else unexpected and even more disturbing. There were photographs in the drawer Amalia had just opened, and the one on top had an inscription on it that said: "To Estela."

Meanwhile, with no prompting from anyone, Amalia had made another deduction. "Do you think my uncle . . . ? Would he have been capable . . . ? No, impossible! When he was in there writing the letter . . . of having taken the medicine. No, it's not possible. He wouldn't have taken his own life. He was happy."

"No, Amalia," I said, "don't jump to conclusions. We know that this bottle was full yesterday and now it's empty. Later, we'll try to figure out calmly what that might mean."

"For the time being," Canalejas suggested, "why don't you say another rosary?"

Amalia left the office, bumping into the furniture as she went, thoroughly disconcerted. A little while later, we could hear her voice reciting "In the name of the Father, the Son, and the Holy Ghost," in a perfectly relaxed tone.

"Do you think Ramón could have committed suicide?" Canalejas asked.

"There's no way of telling," I answered, "until we know what it says in the letter he wrote."

"I must have some idea before then," he said to me, "because I certified that Ramón died of natural causes. Don't you think it might be worthwhile to retract and request an autopsy?"

It was a very difficult decision to make because, after all, if Ramón had committed suicide, there was no point in making it public and creating a scandal. There were a number of reasons in favor of letting him be buried as one who had died a natural death.

"What does seem evident," I said, "is that whether Ramón drank the zafia water because he wanted to or without knowing it, he must have done it in this office."

We looked around trying to find a clue. The plans and calculations that Marcos had brought were on the small table. There was a smell of cigarettes in the room but the bottles and ashtrays had been removed. I asked Canalejas, "Do you think pure zafia water could be swallowed?"

"Not the amount Ramón drank. It would have made him vomit."

"That is to say, he would have had to mix it with something, such as . . ."

"Mineral water, which Lucero brought him, according to Amalia."

"Let's have a look around the kitchen," I suggested.

There were four men in the corridor delivering a huge wreath that said "Harvesters' Union," in letters made of daisies. Alfonso was showing them where to place it. As we went past the living room, I heard Amalia saying Virgo Veneranda again. Zenaida was in the kitchen washing cups. We had to present our condolences to her before we could ask her the questions we wanted to.

"It seems, Zenaida, that last night, when Ramón was talking to señor Marcos for a while, señorita Lucero brought them something to drink. Could you tell us which glass was Ramón's?"

Zenaida pointed to one of the glasses in the cupboard. Canalejas held it up to his nose and made a sign indicating that it didn't smell of anything.

"You washed it?" I asked.

"No, don Pepe. I only wash glasses when they are dirty and this one was clean. The boss didn't drink any mineral water last night. To tell the truth, don Pepe, the boss almost never drank his mineral water at night. The bottle doña Amalia or señorita Lucero took to the office went in and came back out without being touched. That's why I didn't wash the boss's glass, because it was clean."

At that moment I realized what should have been clear to me from the outset. Every night Ramón did what he did at midday—he drank on the sly.

"Let's have a look around the office," I suggested to Canalejas.

We left the kitchen. A delegation from the Casino and some farmhands from The Yoke were entering the house. The wreath from the Harvesters' Union was dwarfed by one from the government of the state of Plan de Abajo. In the office, I went straight to the safe and began to twist the dial. I knew the combination and had no trouble getting it open. I took out the three glasses that were inside and Canalejas and I kept smelling them all, one after another. There was no doubt that none of them had been washed in some time. Two had a slight odor of mezcal and the other, without any doubt, smelled of zafia water. I took out the bottle of mezcal that was also in the safe. We both smelled it and agreed that it smelled of mezcal.

"Let's have another look around the kitchen," I said.

We went to the kitchen. There were many people in the corridor.

"Tell me, Zenaida, where is the bottle señorita Lucero took to the office last night?"

"I threw it in the garbage."

"Would you do us a favor, Zenaida," said Canalejas, "and get it out of the garbage?"

Zenaida looked at us in disbelief.

"We need to see the bottle, Zenaida," I said.

"But it's empty."

"It doesn't matter, Zenaida. The doctor and I have to see it."

She fished a Martell cognac bottle from the garbage and had started toward the sink to rinse it out when Canalejas almost snatched it out of her hand. He uncorked it and brought it up to his nostrils. He looked a bit foolish, like a person trying out a new vice. After smelling it, Canalejas passed it to me triumphantly, saying, "Just take a whiff."

As I reached for the bottle I noticed that somebody had thrown coffee grounds into the garbage. I thought it necessary to explain to Zenaida, "It's very important for us to know what this bottle smells of."

It stank to high heaven of zafia water.

"What time did you take this bottle out of the office, Zenaida?" I asked.

"I didn't, don Pepe. Señora Amalia took it out when señor Marcos left. She put it in the dining room next to the dirty ashtray and I brought it into the kitchen when I finished serving the table."

Canalejas and I left the kitchen with the empty bottle and held a conference in the service patio.

"You knew Ramón a lot better than I did," said Canalejas. "What do you make of all this?"

I told him what I was thinking: that Ramón had not committed suicide but had drunk zafia water with cognac, believing it was pure cognac.

"That is to say, somebody put the zafia water into the cognac bottle without Ramón knowing it."

"Exactly."

"That is to say, I should request an autopsy."

"I think it would be advisable."

"Do you feel we ought to tell the family beforehand what we suspect?"

"You decide. You're the doctor."

Canalejas made up his mind. "Let's call them together, then."

I never envied him less. We started toward the living room.

"The most disturbing thing about this case," he said to me, "is that one of those people we are going to see in there in a moment is probably the one who put the zafia water into the cognac."

"That's just it."

A thought had been going round and round in my mind since a while before, giving me no peace. Marcos had known for some days where the zafia water was kept, since he had seen the photos inscribed "To Estela" in the same drawer.

If I had never envied Canalejas less when I thought of the task he had to undertake, I never admired him more as I observed him at work. Without the other mourners taking notice, he got "Handsome's" children and "The Gringo" together in the office. He locked the door and then, picking up the little blue bottle with the label of my pharmacy on it, he explained how he and I thought Ramón had died.

"My uncle, poisoned!" exclaimed Gerardo, incredulously.

Alfonso, who had been sitting, jumped up. Fernando, on the contrary, had to sit down on the arm of Amalia's chair. All "The Gringo" did was to pull up his socks. Amalia refused to believe that Ramón drank cognac when he had been forbidden to. I had to confess that I usually had mezcal with him in the afternoons and that, consequently, there was no reason to doubt that he could have been drinking cognac in the evening with Marcos.

"Then," said Amalia, "Marcos and my uncle were deceiving me."

"Marcos deceived us all," Alfonso said. "He claimed he was a mining consultant and had an office on Palma Street. A lie. There is no mining consultant's office on Palma Street. He said he had an International pickup truck. Also untrue. No truck of that make is registered under the name of Marcos González. He said he had done studies for El Monte Mining Company. False again. That company never employed a private consultant by the name of Marcos González. We all heard him make those statements but I took the trouble to note everything down and have it all checked out by our credit investigators. The results show that Marcos came to Muérdago to fool us. And he did."

I could have added the matter of the cryolite samples that came from two mines, but I said nothing.

There was a knock on the door. I opened it. It was Zenaida.

"There's a man outside who wants to talk to don Ramón."

"Tell him he can't talk to don Ramón because he's dead."

"That's what I told him but he doesn't want to leave. He says he has to talk to a member of the family and that it's very urgent. He gave me this card."

It was a calling card with the raised seal of Mexico, on which it said "Francisco Santana Esponda," and, in one corner, "Inspector, Criminal Investigation Division."

Alfonso came over to me and asked, "What's going on?"

"The police have arrived," I said, handing him the card.

Santana Esponda was wearing a gabardine suit and carried a briefcase. He had a gold tooth.

"Good morning," he said, as he entered the office. "Excuse me. I won't take much of your time."

He set his briefcase down on the small table, opened

it, took out several copies of the same photograph, and handed them around.

"I would like you to tell me if you recognize this individual," he said.

I looked at the photograph, which was an enlargement and somewhat blurred. It was of a woman and a bearded man in bathing suits, drinking beer.

"The Gringo" was the first to say, "It's Marcos."

"Is he a relative of you people?"

"By marriage," Gerardo assured him, returning the photograph. "A cousin by marriage."

"It is my duty to inform you," said Santana, "that we have proof that he is implicated in the Globo fire."

"Oh, how dreadful!" exclaimed Amalia.

"Just exactly at the time you were arriving, Inspector," said Alfonso, "I was saying to my brother and the doctor and to don Pepe here and my brother-in-law, that Marcos González is a criminal."

"Have you any idea where I might find him?" asked Santana.

I didn't say a word, the Tarragonas looked at one another, and then "The Gringo" stood up.

"I know where Marcos is," he said. "I'll take you to him right now if you like, Inspector."

12

Ramón's wake, which started out so solemn and formal, suddenly turned into one of the most notorious scandals we ever had in Muérdago. The ambulance that was going to transport the body to the hospital for the post mortem, and the hearse that brought the de luxe casket Alfonso had ordered by telephone from Pedrones, arrived at the door and double-parked at the same time. In the corridor, which was packed, the mourners squeezed up against one another, first to let the coffin pass—looking at it with reverence since it was pearl gray with silver handles—and a second time so that the body, coming in the opposite direction, could get by. It was identifiable as such because it was covered by a sheet, the coroner having disarranged the shroud, and because two attendants from the General Hospital morgue, well-known in Muérdago, were carrying the battered stretcher on which it lay. Shock-waves of curiosity swept through the assemblage.

Lucero, with whom we had not discussed what had happened, looked at the bundle being carried out the front door, realized it was Ramón's body, and fainted. I wanted to help her but when I finally managed to get to her, some women were already holding smelling salts under her nose.

In the corridor I saw Amalia, who, not knowing that her daughter had fainted, was addressing various people saying: "Thank you very much for having come here to share our grief on this sad occasion. Dr. Canalejas wishes to have a doubt cleared up in his mind and has requested that an autopsy be performed on my uncle. As soon as we ourselves know when the funeral is to take place we will notify you without fail."

Paco of the Casino came over to me and said, "Tell me if I'm off, Pepe: The new nephew killed Ramón and skipped. Hasn't that got it?"

I pretended not to hear and went into the office. Alfonso was talking on the telephone and Gerardo was rifling one of the desk drawers. He jumped when he saw me enter, and said, "I was looking for matches."

I sat down in one of the armchairs. Alfonso was saying, ". . . under very suspicious circumstances . . . I would like to request, *licenciado*, that you be good enough to step in and see to it that we are given due respect in the proceedings. You will recall that my uncle Ramón was a leading citizen."

I sat there as Alfonso spoke to the governor, the mayor, the notary, the chief of police, and the editor of the *Sol de Abajo*. He asked one or another of them for moral support, for an appointment, or simply to violate the Constitution or some regulation. Meanwhile Gerardo came across a thousand-peso note, which he furtively pocketed, thinking I wasn't looking.

"Majorro will be here at three o'clock," Alfonso said, "to take depositions."

He dialed another number, spoke to the chief of the military zone, and asked for his help.

"What do you need help from the head of the military zone for?" I asked him when he had hung up.

"It's not very likely that we will be needing it," he explained, "but those people always feel flattered when a person like me asks them for a favor."

Gerardo had come across Ramón's watch. Alfonso said, "All of us know that watch, Gerardo, so put it back where you found it."

Fernando came into the office. He seemed bewildered.

"I don't understand," he said. "I was just notified that Marcos left the Land Rover in a garage last night with instructions to deliver it to me. He even paid for the service in advance."

"Are you sure there isn't some part missing?" asked Alfonso.

"Apparently it's in perfect condition. I don't understand."

The three brothers seemed put out.

I got up and left the office. The corridor was nearly vacant. The people who had been acting as though they were never going to leave, suddenly disappeared at two o'clock on the dot. I imagined the downtown bars filled with mourners speculating along similar lines as Paco of the Casino. I stepped between the wreaths and went into the living room. Somebody had opened the windows to ventilate the place. I want over to a balcony and looked out. Remnants typical of the aftermath of an accident or fight were on the street: the man with the wooden tub selling crackerjacks; three farmhands from The Yoke sitting on the curb; the young ladies who lived across the street out on their balconies; several women from neighboring houses standing in the doorway of _La Mascota_, a little candy store, gossiping with the proprietress, who appeared to be pantomiming a corpse covered with a sheet. Suddenly I felt a presence in the living room, turned, and saw Lucero, who was picking up the used cups. She was extremely pale.

"You look very tired, Lucero," I said to her. "Why don't you go and lie down?"

"I'd rather keep busy. It saves me from thinking."

I figured she was right and helped her collect the cups.

Zenaida had made a pile of sandwiches and put them on the dining room table together with some bottles of beer. We were eating silently when Majorro, the agent from the district attorney's office, arrived with a stenographer, installed himself in the living room, and began taking depositions. He interviewed Amalia first, followed by Lucero, and then "Handsome's" three sons, one by one. I was called sixth, after having finished the crossword puzzle in *Fuensanta* magazine.

"Good afternoon, don Pepe," said Majorro when I entered the room. "Have a seat, please."

Majorro had turned on the crystal chandelier that consumed a lot of electricity. I sat down in one of the uncomfortable chairs.

"Will you be good enough to give us your personal data, so my colleague here can take note of them."

When I had completed this requirement, Majorro said, "I understand you were the one who brought the individual to this house."

I realized that the "individual" was Marcos.

Majorro went on, "I would appreciate your explaining your reason for having taken that step."

Obviously Amalia had told him how she had refused to let Marcos in when he arrived at the house the first time. I said that it had seemed to me the most natural thing in the world that Marcos should want to see his uncle, and for that reason I invited him to spend the night in my house and brought him to Ramón's the next day.

"Didn't it seem suspicious that the individual should have shaved in the morning in an effort to alter his appearance?"

"No, señor Majorro, it seemed to me like a very good idea, because he looked untidy with that beard of his."

"I must ask, don Pepe, that you address me as *licenciado*."

"Certainly, *licenciado*."

"According to other declarations, the individual appeared at the house carrying a poncho and a book. A botanical book, it seems. Did you see that book?"

"Naturally, *licenciado*. I gave it to Marcos. Its name is *The Medicinal Herb Garden*, and the author is Dr. Pantoja."

"What was your motive, don Pepe, in giving such a book to a person whom you had not seen in many years?"

"It seemed to me that Marcos was a very intelligent young man and could make good use of it, not because I was aware of any special interest on his part in botany."

This reply seemed to satisfy Majorro. "Very well," he said, and added in a much more pointed manner, "and can you tell me if there is any reference in that book to zafia water?"

I realized that, without intending to, I had put Marcos in a spot. There was nothing for me to do but tell the truth. "Yes. There is a whole chapter on zafia water in *The Medicinal Herb Garden*, describing how it is prepared, what the dosages are, and its effects."

In addition to what the stenographer wrote, Majorro made notes on a pad.

"Thank you, don Pepe," he said.

And he told me I could leave.

It was dusk when I got home. My wife, who had left Ramón's house early, was sure I would be starving to death, and had prepared a huge meal. When I sat down to the plate of macaroni before me, I realized that the stupid statement I had made to Majorro had taken my appetite away. As I was looking at the macaroni, Jacinta said to me, "I found this note between the flower pots next to the front door."

She handed me one of the folded papers Ramón used to send to me with Zenaida. On seeing that bit of paper, the idea that Ramón was dead hit me harder than when I saw the body. I realized that I had in my hand the last message I would ever be receiving from Ramón. I unfolded it and read: *The birdie came back, but a little delayed. All matters pending have been arranged. Don't bother doing what I asked you to. Ramón.*

Then I understood what had happened. Zenaida must have arrived at the house too late, and nobody answered the door when she knocked. Thinking we were asleep and not daring to disturb us, she pushed the paper under the door, where it remained between the flower pots. I left the house in the morning without noticing it. If I had found the message in time, it would have saved me the trip to The Cauldron, I thought. Now, however, as I write this several months later, I am glad I didn't because it was a good thing I went.

"I don't feel like having any supper," I said, and pushed the plate of macaroni aside.

"Sometimes," Jacinta said to me, "sadnesses like this give a person an appetite, and sometimes they can take it away."

When I left the dining room, she was eating the macaroni she had heated up for me. I went out to the patio to look at the plants, and stopped at the brumidora, which at night gives off a very strong odor like that of rue. Thoughts of Marcos, *The Medicinal Herb Garden*, Inspector Santana, and the photographs he had showed us ran through my mind. I realized that although Marcos had made me feel distrustful of him at various times, he did not seem like a terrorist to me, and even less a poisoner. I decided that what had happened was enough for one day and that I would bring it to a close by retiring earlier than usual.

As I was undressing in my bedroom, I found the two receipts from the hotel at The Cauldron in my pocket. I concluded that Marcos's call to Ramón's house at five-thirty was frankly very strange. He must have gotten through to somebody, because the conversation lasted four minutes. He probably made the call to notify his uncle that he would be late, but nobody had told Ramón, even though they all knew he was anxious for news of Marcos.

I went to the telephone with the other receipt in my hand and dialed the number that was noted down on it. A man's voice answered, "Half Moon Beach, Hotel Aurora."

I hung up without saying anything, went back to my room, and put the two receipts and Ramón's note brought by Zenaida into the drawer of my night table, after which I lay down on my back, my hands clasped under my head, and thought for a while. Jacinta came in, got undressed, and slipped into bed alongside me.

"I don't understand a thing," I said, as I turned out the light.

"You don't understand a thing about what?" Jacinta asked.

The following day as I was watering the mandíbulos, there was a knock on the door. It was 8:15 in the morning. Jacinta was in the kitchen preparing breakfast, so I answered. It was Santana and Majorro. They said they were very sorry to be bothering me so early.

"Come in," I said to them. "Have you had breakfast?"

"We don't like to impose, don Pepe," said Majorro.

I asked Jacinta to fix more sausage and eggs.

"Just look, Inspector!" said Majorro, who is an amateur poet, "What a beautiful house don Pepe has. If I lived here, I would be writing like Amado Nervo."

Santana, who was holding onto his briefcase, seemed impatient but said nothing until we had finished breakfast and Jacinta had left the dining room with the dirty dishes. He said, "Yesterday you didn't tell us, don Pepe, either me or *licenciado* Majorro, that you had been to The Cauldron."

I stalled, brushing some crumbs off my shirt; Majorro coughed, cleared his throat, and spit into a bandanna handkerchief; Santana put a receipt on the table just like the one in my night-table drawer, showing that I had made a telephone call from The Cauldron hotel to Ramón's house at 8:00 A.M.

"I didn't say anything to you or *licenciado* Majorro yesterday," I answered, "because neither you nor *licenciado* Majorro asked me where I had been."

"But you knew, don Pepe, that I was looking for Marcos González Alcántara, alias 'El Negro.'"

"Yes, *licenciado*, but I also heard Jim Henry offer to take you to him. I wasn't able to do that for the simple reason that I don't know where Marcos González is."

"Would you be good enough to tell us now, don Pepe, what the purpose was of your going to see that individual at The Cauldron?"

I told them the truth, which coming from my own lips, sounded very unconvincing, particularly the part about my not having found the note Zenaida had pushed under the door in which Ramón told me that there was no need for me to go looking for Marcos, and so forth. When I had finished my story, Santana looked as though he was satisfied, and he said, "I guess I had better luck than you."

"You found Marcos?" I asked.

"That remains to be seen," Santana answered.

Majorro added, "Inspector Santana came across something we would like you to identify. Would it be too much to ask you to come along with us, don Pepe? It's a matter of two or three hours."

"Wherever you say," I replied, standing up.

I agreed to go with them partly because I had no

choice and partly because I was very curious as to what Santana had come up with.

Santana had a big, battered car that he drove very recklessly at high speed. The direction he took indicated that we were going to The Cauldron, as I expected. I sat between them. After riding in silence for a while, I decided to make conversation. "What branch of the government does the division you work for come under?" I asked Santana.

He launched into a long bureaucratic explanation by which he gave me to understand that the Division of Investigation is practically the President's right hand.

"Tell us about some of the cases you have investigated," I asked him.

He described various investigations, among them the case of the paymaster of a government company who disappeared with fifty thousand pesos. The theft took place in Los Mochis, not far from the U.S. border, and he captured the thief a week later in Tuxtla Gutiérrez, near the Guatemalan border.

"When I collared him," Santana said, "he offered me five thousand pesos. 'Excuse me,' I said to him, 'but I'm high-grade.' It was practically an insult. That character is in the can now. He got five years for fraud. The interesting thing about the case, don Pepe, is that this fellow had over a million pesos in his hands only a week before the theft. He didn't touch it. And a week later, he took off with fifty thousand he had in his drawer. It seems he was mixed up with a woman and had to get out of town. 'If you had skipped with the million,' I told him when I brought him in, 'not even God Almighty would have caught up with you.' Half a million pesos, don Pepe . . . there's not a policeman alive who could resist it. Do you get my drift, don Pepe?"

"Yes, yes, I got it," I said.

Majorro added this rider: "People expect the police force to be incorruptible, but why should it be, if we are all only human?"

Instead of driving toward the hotel, Santana took the road to the mine. There was a policeman at the entrance to the half-ruined house who stood up when he saw us arriving, jammed on his cap, and straightened his uniform. I recognized "Teeth," a familiar figure among the members of the Muérdago police force. He is fat, his face is covered with pimples, and he is thought to be mentally retarded. He was listening to Mexican country music on the radio. He snapped to attention when we approached but did not turn off the radio.

"All's well, *licenciado*," he said to Majorro.

"If you'd be good enough, don Pepe," said Santana, "come this way with us."

He went off along a path with me following and Majorro behind. It was rather a steep climb and we had to stop to catch our breath when we came to the top of the first incline. I could see "Teeth" busy sucking on a piece of sugar cane. The voice of Pedro Infante now re-echoed from the hills around. We continued walking. The path was treacherous, sometimes running around a hill on the same level, sometimes taking off with determination up a steep slope, and at other times suddenly plunging downward for no apparent reason. I observed that the flora at The Cauldron was more varied than one would think. Besides the huisaches and garambullo cactuses that abounded, there was palo dulce and palo prieto, some casahuates, pitayos, nopalillo de San Antonio, baldana, yerba andariega, and three types of corínfulas. As we advanced, the terrain changed color, first to whitish, then to reddish, and finally to bluish-gray. Suddenly, as we were going uphill, I heard a roaring noise that did not seem to coincide with my panting or the pounding in my temples. At first I did not know what it was, but then I realized that it must be the sound of The Boiler. A policeman and a farmer who were playing cards under a huisache got to their feet when they saw us. Santana looked around when we came to a turn, and warned me, "Watch your step."

We had come to a deep pool out of which rose a cloud of steam. The ground was slippery. Walking around the edge, we reached the outlet of the rivulet where the water pours out of the spring. Santana stopped and the policeman and the farmer came over to join us, the latter shaking hands with us. Santana waited for me to wipe off my glasses, which had clouded over from the steam, and when I put them back on, he said, "Look," and pointed to the bed of the stream.

It took me a moment to figure out what Santana wanted me to see. Finally, I was able to distinguish two strange brown objects resting on the green slime at the bottom of the stream.

"Can you make that out?"

"Yes."

"Do you recognize those shoes?"

"They are Marcos's Argentine boots," I said without hesitation.

"Did you hear that, *licenciado*?" Santana asked Majorro, who had finally arrived, out of breath. Majorro nodded and Santana said to me, "We'll take what you just said, don Pepe, as a formal declaration before the district attorney."

"But what is this all about?" I asked.

Santana and Majorro took me aside to where the policeman and the farmer would not be able to overhear us.

"This fellow," said Santana indicating the farmer, "is from The Cauldron and is called El Colorado. He is the one who found the boots. He says the body is in the pool."

"What body?"

"The body of Marcos González, alias 'El Negro,'" said Majorro.

Santana explained, "It seems that Marcos González returned to The Cauldron on Thursday night. We don't know if he threw himself into The Boiler intentionally or if he slipped and fell in. In any case, it's just a matter of dragging to find the body and close the file."

He seemed quite satisfied.

"They are waiting for you at the notary's," Jacinta said when I got home.

"What do they want me for?" I asked.

"It seems that *licenciado* Zorrilla is going to read Ramón's will and he doesn't want to open it until you are present."

I went to the bathroom to take care of my lesser wants. As I was urinating, I repeated Santana's words aloud: "It's just a matter of dragging to find the body and close the file."

They sounded even stranger to me.

Those around the table in the notary's office looked at me ill-humoredly when I arrived because they had been waiting an hour for me. Sitting there were "Handsome's" four children but not the wives, "The Gringo," stinking up the room with his cigar, and Lucero, being Ramón's only grandniece who was of age.

Zorrilla had met me in the waiting room. "Canalejas and Paco of the Casino are here," he explained, "because they were witnesses when Ramón made his will."

"Why do I have to be here?" I asked.

"Because Ramón told me you were to be the executor."

I sat down between Lucero and "The Gringo." Zorrilla closed the door and took a seat at the head of the table. He said, "The act we are about to celebrate is fully legal."

"Of course, *licenciado*," said Gerardo, who is a judge.

"When a person dies under circumstances suggesting that death was not natural, it is the notary's prerogative to decide whether the will shall be opened immediately or whether to wait for the results of the investigations in course. In this case, I have decided to open the will now, because I consider that the document we are about to read may contain a clue to the mystery the authorities are trying to clarify. Are there any objections to my opening the will?"

"On my part, none," said Gerardo.

"It seems to me," said Alfonso, "that the decision you have reached is the correct one. Don't you think the same, boys?" he asked, looking around.

"Yes," all the presumed heirs, except Lucero, answered.

Apparently the Tarragonas couldn't wait to find out what Ramón had left them. I spoke up. "I would like to know if an invitation was sent to the other presumed heir or an attempt made to send one."

There was silence. Alfonso looked at me as though he did not understand what I had said.

"Other presumed heir? To whom are you referring, don Pepe?"

"To Marcos."

Alfonso seemed to be recalling at that moment an almost forgotten person.

"Ah, but Marcos is not a presumed heir. Did anybody ever hear my uncle say he was going to leave anything to Marcos? I never did."

"Nor I," said Amalia.

"He was Ramón's nephew," I explained.

"Yes, but by marriage," Gerardo pointed out.

"He is Ramón's sole heir," said Paco of the Casino. "I have laid fifteen thousand pesos in bets that the boy will get everything."

There was another silence.

"In any case," said Zorrilla, "the person you just mentioned was not invited, nor did I attempt to reach him."

"That is what I wanted to know," I said, acting as though I were satisfied.

With great solemnity, Zorrilla had Canalejas and Paco of the Casino verify that their signatures were on the envelope and that the wax seals had not been broken. When this requirement had been fulfilled, he broke the seals, opened the envelope, took out the paper inside it, and began to read: "I appoint as executor, attorney, and agent in charge of carrying out my will in the distribution of my assets, my friend of many years' standing, José Lara, and stipulate that the sum of one hundred thousand pesos shall be paid over to him in compensation for the trouble he will be occasioned. . . ."

"The will begins very well," said Gerardo. "Don Pepe is worthy of our fullest confidence."

". . . To my servant Zenaida, who looked after me and my wife Leonor so faithfully for many years, I leave the house in the San José section and two hundred thousand pesos in cash, so that she may live out her remaining years peacefully. . . ."

"Only fair, only fair!" said Amalia. "I'm glad my uncle remembered Zenaida."

". . . To my grandniece Lucero, to whom I owe the few pleasures I have had in the last months, because she played chess with me, I leave the one million one hundred thousand pesos in my savings account in the Banco de la Lonja. . . ."

"Lucero, you must come to the bank tomorrow without fail," Alfonso said, "so you can make the transfer without paying tax."

Lucero burst out crying.

". . . To my niece Amalia, who sacrificed herself for

my sake by coming to live in my house and looking out for my health even more carefully than my doctor himself, I leave the cut-glass chandelier in the parlor. . . ."

There was silence.

"And what else?" asked "The Gringo."

"Nothing else," Zorrilla answered, and went on reading. "To my nephew Alfonso, I leave my leather desk blotter. . . ."

"What!" said Alfonso. "Are you sure it doesn't say portfolio?"

". . . To my nephew Gerardo, I leave the desk itself of which he is so fond. . . .To my nephew Fernando, I leave my saddle that is kept at The Yoke. . . .To my nephew by marriage, James Henry, I leave the ashtray with my initials. . . ."

"The Gringo" said something in English that I didn't understand.

The notary went on with the reading. "To my nephew Marcos, I leave my share of the profits of the Covadonga mine he discovered, and which he will operate. . . .The rest of my assets, which total approximately sixteen and a half million pesos, I leave as a fund for the Casino of Muérdago. . . ."

At this point in the reading, Gerardo and Fernando were on their feet and Alfonso was opening the door. I leaned over to Lucero, who had stopped crying, to ask her, "Can you tell me if Marcos was wearing his Argentine boots when he came back to the house on Friday?"

"No," she said without hesitation. "He bought new shoes."

When I returned home, Jacinta asked me, "What was in the will?"

"Pure craziness."

I hung my hat on the rack and went to my bedroom, opened the little drawer in my night table, took out one of the receipts, went to the telephone, and dialed the number. The same male voice answered, "Half Moon Beach, Aurora Hotel."

"Tell me, how do I get there?"

13

Anyone who wants to get from Muérdago to Ticomán must take three buses, travel twelve hours, lose four hours in Mezcala, eat lunch at six in the evening and supper at midnight. When I got off the bus at the Ticomán terminal, I felt the blast of heat and had to take off my vest—this happened even though I had on the lightest suit I own—and when I went out into the street, I felt even hotter, and had to take my jacket off. I walked over to the port. It was 7:30 in the morning, the sea was calm, and two shrimp boats were anchored in the bay. I could see pelicans flying overhead in the distance. I went to the dock and asked a man who was cleaning fish where the launch to Half Moon Beach was.

"It's that one," he said, pointing to a boat with an awning and benches, named *La Lupita*. "Leaves at nine."

It matched the description the manager of the Aurora Hotel had given me. I went back to the wharf and sat down in one of the restaurants that was open, the name of which was La Reina de Ticomán, and ordered some breakfast. I stayed there until nine o'clock because it was a pleasant place and well-cooled. *La Lupita* weighed anchor at ten. The rest of the passengers consisted of a black family of four who were going to spend the day on the beach.

"Today is my day off," the father, who was a baker, told me.

I must have looked suspicious: an old man with a vest, jacket, hat, necktie, and no bathing suit.

"Are you going to stay at the Beach?" the boatman asked me.

"I'm trying to locate some friends," I told him.

I described Marcos and his wife as best I could, but the boatman did not recall having seen them.

"There's so many," he told me. "Hardly a day goes by that I don't carry somebody over to the Aurora Hotel."

The crossing took an hour. We went from the bay into a nearby cove. We saw the mountains retreat a little, then come closer again. The sea was like a sheet of glass. The small boy who helped the boatman stood in the prow, then jumped into the water with the rope and pulled on it until the launch was aground. The passengers took their shoes off to wade to shore.

The beach was, in fact, in the shape of a half moon, with a border of coconut palms. There were fishermen's huts, two rotting canoes, some nets, a boy casting a line, and a couple of dogs.

"The Aurora Hotel is over there," the boatman told me.

It was a masonry building that stood on a hill.

"What time do you make the return trip to the port?" I asked.

"At three o'clock."

I began to walk along a path covered with thistles. The tabachines were in flower. By the time I reached the hotel porch, I was soaked in sweat. The floor was made of dark-red tiles, like the hotel at The Cauldron. I went through the vestibule to the office.

"Are you the person who called on the telephone?" the man behind the desk asked.

Since he had told me he was the manager, I took out a hundred-peso bill.

As at The Cauldron, there was no trouble getting

information, but, as at The Cauldron also, the manager told me that Marcos wasn't at the hotel. However, he informed me, as well, that somebody had telephoned on Thursday to make a reservation in the name of Angel Valdés and wife, but had never appeared.

"Are you sure?" I asked the manager.

For another hundred pesos he showed me the register. There was really nothing to check. Nobody had registered at the hotel since Friday. I realized that the boatman had exaggerated and that business at the Aurora Hotel was as bad as at The Cauldron hotel. I realized also that the travelling, the loss of sleep, and the two hundred pesos I had given the manager had all been wasted.

"Let me have a beer, then," I said to the manager.

He wouldn't charge me for it. I sipped it sitting in one of the canvas chairs on the porch, and soon fell asleep. When I opened my eyes there was a gray boat in the cove.

"What's that boat?" I asked the manager.

"A government cutter."

"Let me have a mezcal."

A cool breeze had sprung up. I put on my vest right then, and my jacket before boarding La Lupita. The return crossing was very different from the first trip. The ocean had become choppy and the baker's wife got seasick and vomited; the government boat left Half Moon Beach after we did and was already at the wharf when we arrived.

It had gotten cloudy and begun to drizzle, it was cold, the time was four-thirty, and the Mezcala bus was scheduled to leave at six. I went over to La Reina de Ticomán again. When I sat down, I realized I was hungry, and ordered some food. It was twenty minutes of six; I had finished my second cup of coffee, paid the check, and was about to get up from the table when I saw a woman walk by in the street wearing a poncho to protect her from the rain. It was Marcos's poncho.

I went out to the street and had to run a little to catch up with her.

"Excuse me, señorita!" I called out to her.

She turned around in alarm. She was very pretty. Not only was she pretty, but it was the same woman whose photograph Santana had showed us. I had no time to invent a lie and told her the first thing that occurred to me: "I'm looking for Marcos."

I could tell from her expression that she knew a Marcos. I didn't give her a chance to deny it.

"My name is José Lara, I'm a friend of Marcos's and I must talk to him."

She looked at me suspiciously, but I must have inspired confidence, because she finally said to me, "Marcos is in the hospital."

"What's the matter with him?"

"He had a very bad case of poisoning and nearly died."

It wasn't until then that the idea occurred to me that Marcos and Ramón must have been drinking from the same bottle.

"Take me to him," I asked the woman. "It's urgent that I see him."

On the way, she told me that Marcos had fallen asleep on the bus when they left Mezcala, and when she tried to wake him on reaching Ticomán, she realized he was dying.

"I had to take him to the Naval Hospital, since they refused to admit him at the Civil Hospital because they didn't have the necessary equipment to treat him. Today they finally took him off intravenous glucose."

"What does the doctor say?"

"That Marcos was poisoned by some unknown substance he ate or drank. He says that he could just as easily have died, because they didn't know what antidote to give him."

"Did blue spots appear at the bottom of his lower lip?" I asked.

She looked at me in surprise. "How did you know?"

"A friend of mine died of the same thing."

In order to get into the Naval Hospital I had to give my personal data and fifty pesos to the sailor on guard, who let me into a ward in which Marcos was the only patient. He was unrecognizable. He had gotten very thin and was greenish in color. He was asleep but looked like he was dead. His wife went over to him and touched him on the shoulder, finally waking him up.

"There's a man here who wants to talk to you."

Marcos recognized me and smiled weakly.

"How are you feeling?" I asked.

"A little better," he said in a hoarse voice.

"I have a number of things to tell you. Do you want to hear them now or would you rather I came back tomorrow?"

"Now."

I was so happy to have finally found the man I was looking for! Who would ever have imagined that the next moment was going to be the most distressing moment of my life? First I heard the door open, and when I turned around I saw Santana and Majorro coming in, followed by several policemen.

Marcos was moved to Muérdago in an ambulance with a doctor and an escort. Marcos's wife and I went in Santana's car. I rode in front between Santana and Majorro, and she sat in back with the policeman. We did not speak during the first part of the trip, but when we stopped at a restaurant on the highway and got out of the car, Santana took me by the arm and said, "Don't hold it against me, don Pepe. I wouldn't like to have to live with that."

"You tricked me," I said, "because I never believed the story that Marcos had fallen into The Boiler. 'It's just a matter of dragging for the body,' you said. A pack of lies!"

"You're right, don Pepe. Forgive us. But *licenciado* Majorro and I knew that when you went to the hotel at The Cauldron you got two slips of paper that you didn't want to show us."

Since I did not want to discuss the matter, I walked away angrily. They came after me.

"I assure you, don Pepe," Majorro said, "that it was the Inspector who insisted that we go to your house that morning the day before yesterday. Isn't that so, Inspector?"

"Yes, it's so. But, don't be angry, don Pepe. It was thanks to you that everything came out so well. Now the *licenciado* can close his file and I can close mine. Let's all go and have a drink to celebrate this victory of justice."

I looked at them as witheringly as I was capable of doing. These biweekly-paycheck bureaucrats—I thought to myself—don't care about anything but closing files.

"Thank you very much, no," I told them cuttingly.

They went to the restaurant where they ordered roast suckling pig. I stayed at the door walking back and forth, but I was hungry and thirsty and ended up going to the bar and ordering a sandwich and a beer.

"Join us, don Pepe," called Majorro from their table.

"No, thank you," I repeated, and then said to the waitress, "Bring me two sandwiches and two beers."

When she brought them, I took one of each to the car for Marcos's wife, who was alone in the back seat of the car. The policeman had handcuffed her ankles and gone for something to eat. When I approached her she was still being unfriendly, looking out of the window in the opposite direction.

"Here. I brought you this," I said to her.

She turned around, looked disdainfully at the sandwich and beer and at me—I could tell even though it was dark—and said to me, "No, thank you very much."

I went back to the restaurant, sat down with the two officials, and accepted the tequila and roast suckling pig.

The bells were ringing for six o'clock Mass as I was entering my house. Jacinta woke up when I went into the bedroom.

"How did it go?" she asked.

"Bad. All I did in Ticomán was make a damn fool of myself."

I got into bed and slept soundly. When I woke up it was getting dark again. Jacinta had come into the room and turned on the light.

"*Licenciado* Zorrilla is in the living room," she said to me. "This is the third time he has been here to see you."

"Now what does he want?"

"To talk to you as soon as you are awake."

"I'm awake."

I sent Zorrilla the key to the liquor closet so he could have a drink while I washed my face and put on my bathrobe and slippers. When I came into the living room, I found him jiggling his foot up and down, a sign that he was nervous. He stood up when he saw me, and said, "Pepe, I sure am glad to see you."

"What's going on?"

"I received a letter from Ramón this morning."

"A letter from Ramón?"

He took it out of his pocket and gave it to me. As soon as I saw the envelope I realized it was the letter that Ramón had written on Thursday night and Zenaida had mailed. Inside the first envelope there was a letter and a second sealed envelope.

"Read it," Zorrilla said to me.

It said:

> *Dear Pablo Zorrilla:*
> *I want to ask a very big favor of you: Add to the will I made the other day the provision you will find enclosed, and cancel all clauses that contradict it. Do not think that I am feeling ill. I just want to leave things in order. Excuse me for all the trouble.*
>
> *Ramón Tarragona (signed)*

"Is this valid?" I asked.

"It should have two witnesses."

I went to the door and shouted, "Jacinta!"

When Jacinta was there, Zorrilla opened the second envelope and read: "Having had a lengthy conversation with my nephew Marcos González Alcántara, with whom I am more pleased every day and who seems to me to be a worthy person, I have decided to change my last will as set forth in the document dated (. . . and so forth) and leave everything to him that I had previously left to the Casino."

"Frankly," said Zorrilla, removing his glasses, "this second will makes more sense than the other one. Leaving sixteen and a half million to the Casino really seemed out of line."

"Of course," added Jacinta, "it's much more natural to have left it to a relative."

"Do you people know where Marcos is?" I asked.

"He's in jail. He is under suspicion, among other things, of having poisoned Ramón."

"Oh, how ungrateful of him!" exclaimed Jacinta. "What a dreadful thing."

"If it is proved that he is guilty," Zorrilla warned, "the second will automatically becomes null and void."

The thing that was worrying me then was not whether the second will was null or in force but the fact that its content constituted the only known motive for Marcos's having poisoned Ramón.

"Am I still the executor?" I asked.

"That's what the first will provides," said Zorrilla, "and nothing in the second will contradicts that provision."

The next day, when I went to the jail, "Teeth" told me that Marcos was "a good sight better," that he had been taken out of the infirmary where he spent the previous day and was now in a cell. I handed "Teeth" the pass Majorro had gotten for me, which he scrutinized closely without giving any indication that he understood what it said.

"It's a pass," I explained. "It says that I am authorized to enter the prison and visit the prisoner."

"Correct," "Teeth" said, but did not make a move.

"Teeth" and I were alone in the guard room. I took out a twenty-peso bill and handed it to him.

"Step this way, don Pepe," said "Teeth" as he went to take the keys off the hook.

We crossed the courtyard and walked through a passageway that went by the drunk tank. "Teeth" opened the next door and had me go into a dark, damp cell in which there was a toilet that stank abominably. Marcos was lying on a cot, covered with his poncho. Strangely enough, he was pleased to see me.

"Hello, don Pepe," he said, sitting up.

"Teeth" picked up some dirty plates from the floor and left us alone. I sat down on the bed next to Marcos, who said, "The jail food is inedible. I had something sent in from the Universal Hotel but this fat cop who just left ate half of it before it reached me."

I promised to have Jacinta bring him a basket of provisions, and then I started on the matter that concerned me.

"You know that Ramón is dead, don't you?" I asked.

"So they told me."

"And that he was poisoned?"

"Yes, I know that, too."

"You and he were drinking cognac."

"We drank cognac every night. On Thursday, my uncle had more than usual because there wasn't much left in the bottle. I drank two glasses of it and then switched to mezcal. My uncle finished off the cognac."

"That's what saved your life. The cognac was poisoned."

"Just as I thought."

"You knew where they kept the medicine, didn't you?"

"Yes, but I didn't know it was poisonous."

"But you had the *Medicinal Herb Garden* book, which says that zafia water is deadly."

"I never got to that part."

"But you had the book. Somebody saw it in your possession and said so in one of the depositions."

"What you are saying, then, is that I am suspected of having poisoned my uncle?"

"Precisely."

"But we were both poisoned at the same time. I can get a medical certificate to that effect."

"Your story would have been more convincing if you had died and not gotten only a little poisoned, as happened."

"What point could there have been in my poisoning my uncle? What would it have gotten me? He gave me a check for forty thousand pesos that night."

"Do you know that Ramón wrote a second will that

night in which you are named sole heir, apart from a few other minor legacies?"

Marcos covered his face with his hands.

"Do you see, now, that you are in a very bad spot?"

"Don Pepe, I did not kill my uncle."

"I know you didn't, but you are implicated in the Globo fire, and that makes you a very suspicious person."

"I didn't have anything to do with the Globo fire, either."

"In other words, you are being accused of two crimes, neither of which you had anything to do with. That's incredible."

He shrugged his shoulders and, in a fatalistic tone, said, "I come from up in the hills, my father was a loser, everybody calls me El Negro, and the only piece of luck that ever came my way turns out to be proof that I murdered my uncle. Life has handed me a royal screwing. And, if that's not enough, I already loused myself out of my good luck by signing an agreement with my cousins to hand over four-fifths of the inheritance."

"How's that?" I said. "Explain it to me."

When I called to say I wanted to see him, Alfonso had me shown immediately to his private office. He was standing in the doorway waiting for me with his arms out.

"Don Pepe," he said when I went in, "I heard you were the one who made it possible to capture that sonofabitch."

I wasn't able to avoid the embrace. When I stepped away from him and we sat down, I said to him, "I don't know whether Zorrilla has spoken to you about the letter he received."

"What letter did Zorrilla receive?"

"The one Ramón wrote."

Obviously he had heard nothing. I told him that Ramón had written a second will and what it said. His face lit up.

"In that case," he said, "I and the rest of us will get a much larger share than was coming to us under the first will, because we signed an agreement with Marcos to the effect that whatever the four of us and our cousin receive, it will be divided into five equal parts."

"I understand that," I said. "The sad part of the case, however, is that Majorro and Santana are determined to show that Marcos poisoned Ramón, and if they do, it means that the second will becomes null and void."

I admired the promptness with which he grasped the twist the problem had taken.

"But we are not going to permit a couple of cops to dispose of the matter as they see fit."

"Of course not."

"Marcos is a scoundrel without any doubt, but he's not a murderer."

"That's what I thought."

"It seems to me, don Pepe, that my uncle was not murdered but rather he committed suicide."

"He was a very sick man."

"Never mind the sickness, think of the constant humiliation of having to depend upon others to carry out the most ordinary routines of your daily life for you."

"It was a terrible situation for him."

"I have the idea that, although such an act is usually considered sinful, it is forgiven by Our Lord God."

"I have a message that Ramón sent me that Thursday night, which I did not read until Friday when he was already dead and which I cannot figure out."

I handed him the note Zenaida had pushed between the flower pots.

" 'The birdie is back but a little delayed,' " Alfonso

read. "Do you think my uncle might have been referring to the Holy Ghost?"

"It's possible."

" 'All matters pending have been arranged.' This seems open and shut to me. It is the letter of a person who knows he is going to die. It is a suicide note. What's your opinion, don Pepe?"

"It could be interpreted that way."

" 'Don't bother doing what I asked you to.' That escapes me."

"It's something irrelevant."

"Listen, don Pepe, I have a young woman here in the bank who has an incredible facility for imitating other people's handwriting and who is absolutely trustworthy. How about if we were to give her this note and have her write in the corner here where there is a blank space, something like 'Don't blame my death on anybody.' "

"I don't think that's necessary," I answered, taking the paper from him and putting it in my pocket, "particularly since you and I are agreed that Ramón died by his own hand."

"We see eye to eye on that point, don Pepe."

"As executor," I went on, "I must ask you the following question. Would you and your brothers be in a position to liquidate Marcos's share of the inheritance in advance, in cash?"

"Do you consider it an indispensable condition for concluding this matter?"

"Absolutely indispensable."

"In that case, don Pepe, Marcos can count on the cash the moment he needs it. This bank is at his service."

When I left the Banco de la Lonja, instead of walking through the arcade toward home, I went by way of

Sonaja Street toward Ramón's house. I saw "The Gringo" come out slamming the door, get into his car slamming the door again, start the car with a violent jerk, and shoot off. When Zenaida opened the door for me, she commented, "Señor Jim is angry." In a confidential tone, she added, "He found some faces in the trash that Señorita Lucero drew of señor Marcos."

"In the trash?"

"She tore them up herself and threw them in the trash. I took the trash basket out of the trunk room, and brought it into the patio where I met don Jim and he said to me, 'What have you got there?' 'Nothing,' I answered, 'just trash.' He picked up the pieces of the faces and was looking at them. He didn't say anything but he turned very red and went away."

Amalia and Lucero were in their rooms, packing. They came into the corridor when Zenaida told them I had arrived.

"It makes me very sad to have to leave this house," said Amalia, who evidently had not heard about the second will.

"Wouldn't you like a cup of coffee, don Pepe?" Lucero asked.

"No, thanks. I just came for a moment to say hello and to tell you that Marcos is in jail."

"We heard," said Amalia coldly.

Lucero had nothing to say, and I went on talking. "It seems that the meals they serve in the jail are terrible. My wife is going to bring him a basket of food. If you would like to send him something, she could take it."

"I wouldn't send him anything," said Amalia.

"I think I will," said Lucero.

I then left.

On the floor in the hall next to the door of the room occupied by *licenciado* Santana at the Universal Hotel were several empty bottles and a service for two with the leavings of breakfast. A "Do Not Disturb" sign hung from the doorknob. I approached the door and heard voices. I went downstairs and stopped at the desk. Picking up the receiver there, I said to the desk clerk, "Connect me with Room 36."

It was twelve-thirty. When Santana answered, I said to him, "I have a proposition that I believe will interest you and *licenciado* Majorro."

"Does it concern money, don Pepe?"

"If it didn't I wouldn't be calling. Can the two of you meet me at the Casino bar at one o'clock?"

"One-thirty."

"Right."

I hung up.

I went home. Jacinta had set the rocking chair out in the patio and was sitting there darning socks. I put my hands in my pockets and began meandering around while I talked, as though passing on a bit of gossip. "It seems that Lucero drew some portraits of Marcos, then tore them up and threw them in the trash."

On reaching this point, I stopped and looked at my wife. She raised her eyes quickly, dropped them again, and went on with her darning. I waited.

"They had to do," she said finally, without looking at me.

When Jacinta says that two people are "having to do" she means they are having sexual relations.

"How do you know?"

"I noticed them from the roof one afternoon through the window of the room next to the hen coops. I didn't mean to."

She blushed.

When I arrived at the Casino I sat at a table in the farthest corner from the bar, to make sure that no one would hear what I was going to say to Santana and Majorro. They arrived close to two o'clock. I waited for Pedrito, the waiter, to bring their order, and then I began. "What I am about to tell you, I say in my capacity as executor of Ramón Tarragona's will."

They looked at me with respect. I went on. "My principals, the heirs, are interested in avoiding the bad impression that may be caused by the news that Ramón was murdered. They would like to find out if there isn't some way of preventing that from happening."

"*Licenciado* Majorro here has the say," Santana said, "because señor Tarragona's death is a matter outside my competence."

Majorro said, "I am very sorry, don Pepe, but it is too late now. We might have arranged this when we stopped for supper on the way from Ticomán. Now the affair is out of my hands. I have already sent in my report to the main office, the prisoner is already at the disposition of the judge, and all that remains to be done is for him to set the trial date."

"What a pity!" I said, and turned to Santana. "What about you, Inspector? Don't you see some way of closing the file on El Globo without implicating Marcos González and his wife?"

"Don't even ask me that, don Pepe. It's impossible. Take into consideration that the apprehension we were finally able to make the other day represents the end of an investigation that has been going on for months. You have no idea of the amount of work it took to infiltrate the terrorist cell those kids belonged to. You know how those communists are—very distrustful. They only get together among themselves. Just by accident I met a woman who belonged to the group. After I found out what kind of person she was, I insisted on meeting her friends. She didn't want to introduce me to them at first, but finally she took me along with her. Luckily for me, at the meeting I attended, which was precisely in the apartment of those sonsofbitches who are now in jail, the top dog himself, who we've been after, showed up. One Evodio Alcocer. I figured that with this I was going to be able to close my file. No such luck. These two got away. I had to go to Cuévano, come back to Muérdago, then go to Ticomán before I could make the collar, thanks to you, don Pepe. Just imagine what my superiors will say to me if I come back to Mexico City with empty hands."

"I understand your position," I said. I paused a moment and added, resignedly, "I'll tell my principals that there is no way to arrange what they asked me."

"Definitively," said Majorro, "no way."

"Do you know how much they were willing to pay for a satisfactory arrangement of the matter? Three million pesos."

"One moment, don Pepe," said Santana. "What would these people consider a satisfactory arrangement?"

"It has two parts. One, a report that Ramón Tarragona's death was accidental. Two, another report stating that the persons being sought in connection with the Globo fire could not be found and are assumed to have drowned."

"You should have said so to begin with, don Pepe," said Majorro. "I think that the first part, which concerns me, can be arranged, particularly in view of the fact that there is enough money available for commissions. You know how these matters go. A lot of people are involved. They have to be paid for keeping everything confidential. How does it look to you, Inspector?"

"I see some obstacles," said Santana, "but nothing that couldn't be overcome."

They agreed to have the necessary papers ready and to set the prisoner free at that same hour the following day. I promised to have the money ready. When I got up from the table, I left them discussing the details of the operation.

That afternoon, Zenaida brought the pie that Lucero had made for Marcos to my house.

"It has the same sauce she makes for the Agachona pie," she explained to Jacinta, "but there weren't any agachonas, so she used chicken breasts."

When Zenaida left, Jacinta commented, looking down at the pie, "You can see she still loves him."

"Take it to Marcos now when you go," I said.

When my wife came back from the jail, she said to me, "I handed it over to a fat policeman at the entrance."

"So much the better," I said.

The next morning, Canalejas telephoned me. "Did you prepare more zafia water?" he wanted to know.

"I did not and I never intend to again."

"Well, I'm letting you know that there is a policeman known as "Teeth" in the hospital with a bad case of poisoning, and he has blue spots at the base of his lower lip."

"He must have taken the zafia water that's sold in the market by the herb vendors."

"Fortunately it couldn't have been very good zafia water, because all of "Teeth's" hair fell out but he is still alive."

14

For a number of months it seemed as though the story I have told was going to end happily. I never saw Santana or Majorro again. Marcos and his wife went to live in Mezcala and with the half million that was left over opened a regional-type restaurant, where the food is quite good, I have heard, particularly the tamale pie. "Handsome's" four children divided up what was left of the inheritance equitably, according to some, and, according to others, advantageously for Alfonso. Fernando got The Yoke, which is what he always wanted; Gerardo, the houses in the San Antonio section; and Amalia, the Tarragona house; but all of them had to pay interest to Alfonso on the three and a half million that was laid out in cash. In addition, Alfonso kept the stock portfolio, whose value only he knows. Amalia, "The Gringo," and Lucero stayed on in Ramón's house. Lucero put the million pesos she inherited into fixed-interest securities. Zenaida considered that she had worked long enough, and moved to the house Ramón had left her in the San José section. I received punctually the hundred thousand pesos that were coming to me, and turned it over to the Casino as compensation—modest as it was—for the sixteen and a half million that Ramón had left them in the first will. They say I am crazy, but what would Jacinta and I want a hundred thousand pesos for?

In September the probate proceedings were completed and the time came to transfer ownership of the assets. Zorrilla told me that Marcos would have to come to Muérdago to sign the papers. I had his address and got in touch with him. He was glad to comply.

Marcos arrived at the house at night as he had the other time, with a beard and wearing a poncho, but not on foot. He has a car of his own now. His wife was not with him.

"The restaurant business is good, but you can't leave it unattended," he told Jacinta when she asked for his wife.

I had the feeling that this statement was a little too pat to be true and that if he had wanted to bring his wife, he would have brought her.

Marcos was in very good humor and had supper with us. However, when he finished, he said he would like to go out and take a turn around the town. I gave him a key so he could get in anytime he pleased.

"He must be going to have to do with Lucero," Jacinta said when Marcos was gone.

I don't know why that phrase annoyed me so much.

"All right!" I exclaimed, "But what business is it of ours!"

Jacinta and I went to bed at eleven as usual and turned out the light, but neither she nor I fell asleep until Marcos came back, which was considerably after one o'clock. When we heard the door, Jacinta said, in the dark, "Everything in Muérdago closes at midnight, so he must have been in a private home."

Not wishing to comment on this statement, I made a sound as though I were asleep. For a while I wondered whether to get up and see if Marcos was all right, but finally I came to the conclusion that if Marcos let himself be poisoned at this stage of the game, he deserved it. Then I fell asleep.

*   *   *

Marcos appeared in the morning looking well and with a hearty appetite. He had breakfast with us. My wife asked him if he would like to shave. He answered no, and the three of us laughed. Sitting at the table after breakfast, Marcos and I had a conversation that was noteworthy only because we did not mention Ramón, his death, the money, jail, or the poison. At ten-thirty we left the table and went to Zorrilla's office, where our appointment was for eleven o'clock.

All the heirs were punctual. They sat around the table with very solemn expressions, everybody dressed in black, except Marcos who still had his poncho on. Zorrilla had the papers in order and ready for signature. He passed the documents around one by one, showing each person where to sign. When this was done, Zorrilla closed the last ledger and said, "That's all, ladies and gentlemen. Thank you."

Then, in a spontaneous action, the heirs, witnesses, the executor, and the notary rose and embraced one another as though we were at a New Year's Eve party.

Alfonso said, "I would like to invite you all to a picnic I have arranged to celebrate this beautiful fraternal act."

That was the mistake.

Alfonso had chosen The Cauldron. The festivity was planned well ahead of time. He had tables set up under the mesquite trees near the pond. Nothing was lacking. The grandnephews played soccer, "The Gringo" got a rifle out and was practicing target shooting, "Handsome's" sons gathered around them the mariachis that Alfonso had hired and began to cry, we all ate *mole* and drank, and the women, dressed in mourning, couldn't find places to sit because of the ants. The picnic went on for a long time. Suddenly I noticed that

Marcos was not around, nor Lucero. I went walking along the edge of the stream that leads to The Boiler. The sounds could be heard of the soccer ball being kicked, the mariachis singing, and the shots that "The Gringo" was taking at regular intervals at the target. The sun was beginning to set. Suddenly, through the tangle of the huisaches in the distance, I caught sight of Marcos's poncho and felt relieved. The poncho and I approached each other, and not until we were only a few meters apart did I realize that it was Lucero, not Marcos, who was wearing it.

"I thought you were Marcos," I told her.

She smiled and answered, "Marcos gave me his poncho," and continued on her way.

She looked happy and very beautiful. I, still concerned that something might have happened to Marcos, continued walking in the opposite direction until I finally made out another figure among the huisaches. It was Marcos, in shirtsleeves, hands in his pockets, head down, looking into the stream. He was whistling a tune.

When I came up beside him, I said, "It's good to see you."

He looked at me, smiled, then pointed to the bottom of the stream and told me another lie: "That's beryllium salts."

I looked at the bluish deposit on the bed of the stream. Then, as though by mutual accord, we started back in silence to where the picnic was going on. I have no idea how far we walked without noticing that there were no sounds of mariachis, soccer ball, or shots. I remember that I heard the chirping of a cricket and almost simultaneously a woman's shrill scream. Marcos began to run and I followed. I didn't think I could run any further, when I saw Amalia, a handkerchief to her mouth, kneeling alongside a shape on the ground. Several figures were beside her.

They say somebody saw three agachonas flying and pointed to them. Those who were near "The Gringo" say they saw him raise his rifle, and that they thought he was shooting at the agachonas. They say that when they heard the shots and saw that the agachonas were still flying, they looked at the rifle and realized it was pointing in a different direction. Afterwards, they saw the shape on the ground covered with the Santa Marta poncho. They say that when "The Gringo" was told, "It's Lucero," "The Gringo" just shook his head because he couldn't believe it.